The AUTUMN Duchess

A Duchess for All Seasons
Book Four

JILLIAN EATON

This is a work of fiction. Names, characters, places and incidents are either the product of the author's imagination or are used fictitiously, and any resemblance to actual persons, living or dead, business establishments, events, or locales is entirely coincidental.

ISBN: 9781729070666

www.jillianeaton.com

***"ARE YOU GOING TO KISS ME AGAIN?"** Hannah whispered, her eyes two shimmering pools of ash beneath a thick fringe of velvet lashes.*

"Do you want me to?" Evan's voice was hoarse, his blood hot.

"Yes." Her tongue slipped between her lips, drawing his gaze down to her delectable little mouth. A mouth that was all but begging to be tasted. By him. And if that wasn't the most confounding thing on God's green earth he didn't know what was.

Hannah wanted him. The half crippled duke with a disfigured face who'd once been mocked by the entire ton. He didn't know why or how, given as he did not even want himself. But she did.

And he wanted her.

He wanted her more than he'd ever wanted anything in his entire life. More than he'd wanted to walk. More than he'd wanted his father's approval. More than he'd wanted the echoes of Lady Portia's cruel laughter to disappear. And so with a savage growl that was more beast than man, he took what he wanted...

Prologue

Evan did not remember much about the fall.

But he couldn't forget the whispers.

How could he, when from age eight to one and twenty they followed him wherever he went? The whispers were there to greet him in every room he entered. They trailed after him through the hallways. The blasted things even followed him into ballrooms and carriages and the middle of Hyde Park.

Suffice it to say he heard the whispers everywhere. But even worse than the hushed voices, even worse than the gossip and the terse smiles and the horrified gasps, were the pitying stares.

Evan could take the whispers and the staring. He didn't even mind the disgust, for he knew it was well deserved. He had a mirror, hadn't he? He knew what he looked like. Which was why, when children cowered and ladies swooned at the mere sight of him – and not in the good way – he took it all in stride.

But the pity...the pity he could not abide.

Five years had gone by and the back of his neck still

burned with embarrassment and anger whenever he thought of one incident in particular. It had been the night of the Glastonbury ball. A ball he never would have attended if his sweet, ailing mother hadn't begged him to go.

'*You're becoming a recluse Evan,*' she'd cried, her large blue eyes awash with tears. '*Staying in all day and all night. It 'tisn't natural. Especially for a man of your caliber and station.*'

Evan had been tempted to point out that the only thing *unnatural* was his face, but he'd held his tongue. And when his mother began to cry in earnest he'd acquiesced to her request, for despite the hardness in his gaze he'd still had a soft spot in his heart that could not abide a woman's tears. Which was how he found himself standing awkwardly in the shadowy corner of a ballroom while the *ton's* elite swirled by in a pastel blend of ivory gowns and sleek black tailcoats.

Dressed in his own black tailcoat with a crisp white cravat strangling his throat and fawn colored breeches clinging to muscular thighs, he could have almost passed for one of them.

Almost.

Keeping one hand pressed defensively against the puckered flesh on the right side of his face and the other wrapped tightly around a glass of champagne that had already been refilled four times, he failed to notice the petite blonde approaching until she was nearly on top of him.

"Oh!" she exclaimed, round cheeks flushing prettily as she batted her lashes and giggled into the palm of one satin glove. "I am terribly sorry. I fear I did not see you standing there...Your Grace."

Evan stiffened, broad shoulders drawing taut beneath his coat. "You know who I am?"

"Of course," she said, sounding surprised. "Doesn't everyone?"

When his jaw reflexively tightened, pulling at the gnarled scar tissue he was still covering with his hand, she gasped and took an inadvertent step back.

"I - I am terribly sorry. I didn't mean to imply...I just meant that, well, you are a *duke*."

No, he corrected her silently. His *father* had been a duke. And while Evan had technically inherited the title upon his death, he was no more a duke than he was a fish. Or a horse. Or a bloody cloud floating by in the sky.

"Is there something I can help you with, Lady…"

"Portia." Having recovered from her *faux pas*, she offered him a brilliant smile. "Lady Portia James. If I am not mistaken, I believe our mothers attended the same finishing school."

"Indeed," he muttered before he glanced purposefully

over her shoulder in a not-very-subtle indication that he wished for their conversation to be over. Unfortunately, Lady Portia either did not receive the hint or she simply chose to ignore it.

"I can assure you this is quite out of character for me and, well, a bit presumptuous if I am being honest, but…" She hesitated, and Evan felt an unmistakable prickling of desire when she sank her teeth into her plump bottom lip. "Would you care to dance?"

"Dance?" he repeated, so startled by the request that he nearly spilled his champagne. Women – especially women who looked like Lady Portia James – rarely spoke to him, let alone asked him to dance. And yet here she was, standing right in front of him, doing precisely that.

In hindsight, Evan realized he should have known then and there that something was amiss. That Lady Portia, for all of her guilelessness, was not nearly as sweet or innocent as she appeared. But as he'd gazed down into her cornflower blue eyes he had felt something he hadn't felt in a very, very long time. So long, in fact, that it took him a moment to recognize what it was.

Hope.

"All right," he said gruffly, setting aside his flute of champagne on a nearby planter in order to take her arm.

If she noticed his stiff gait as they approached the outskirts of the dance floor she made no mention of it, but he still released a quiet sigh of relief when the quartet of musicians sitting high on a dais began to play a slow, subdued waltz.

Before the fall Evan had been lively and quick; a veritable dervish of athleticism and energy. After it there had been several doctors who had ominously predicted he would never walk again. The late Duke of Wycliffe, determined that his one and only heir would not grow up to be a cripple, had scoured the country until he'd found a physician who told him what he wanted to hear: that his son *would* in fact regain full control of his legs and, with time and exercise, might even make a full recovery.

After years of agonizingly painful therapies that required the use of wooden braces and a barbaric pulley system, Evan *had* managed to walk again. But it was clear, even then, that he'd never be what he once was, much to the duke's everlasting disappointment.

"I apologize." Evan's scars stood out in vivid white contrast against his tanned skin as his face flushed a deep, mottled red when he stepped on Lady Portia's tiny foot for what felt like the hundredth time since they'd begun their waltz. "I – I haven't danced in quite some time."

"It's fine," she assured him, but she couldn't quite disguise the wince of pain that flashed across her features when he tried to turn her in a circle and his leg locked in place, causing their shins to collide.

“This is a mistake.” But when he went to disengage himself she clung fast to his wrist, nails sinking into his sleeve cuff with surprising tenacity.

“I think you’re doing splendidly, Your Grace. Truly,” Lady Portia insisted when Evan made a scoffing sound under his breath. “I can only imagine how difficult it must be for a man of your stature to complete such intricate steps and turns.” Her mouth curved. “Particularly when your partner is significantly lacking in height. I fully accept all of the blame.”

A man of his stature? The way she spoke almost made it seem as if she didn’t notice his physical impairments. But that couldn’t be true...could it?

Again hope stirred inside of Evan’s chest, warming the protective layer of ice he’d used to shield his heart against all of the stares and the whispers and the unwanted pity. Maybe, just maybe, Lady Portia was the sort of woman he’d started to fear did not exist. The kind who could see past his ruined exterior to the man beneath. The kind who saw him for what he was, not for what he was not.

When the dance ended he met her flawless curtsy with an awkward bow, lips twisted in a grimace of discomfort as liquid fire shot up through his ruined leg. The waltz had been more demanding than he’d anticipated, and already he was dreading the inevitable ice bath and stretching that was to come. But such therapies, albeit horrifically painful, were necessary if he wanted to retain the limited range of motion that he still had left. Which he did, particularly now that he had a new incentive to do so.

"Lady Portia, might I have the pleasure of…"

"Of?" she said innocently, batting her lashes at him when his voice trailed away.

"*…of-calling-on-you-tomorrow*?" The words came out in one long, unintelligible sentence that had him inwardly cursing, but thankfully Lady Portia was able to decipher his gibberish. Although she did not give him the answer he wished for.

"I am terribly sorry, Your Grace," she said apologetically. "I would like that very much, but I am afraid I am leaving tomorrow to visit my aunt in Gloucester. Mayhap when I return?"

"Of course." He hesitated, gaze lingering on the curve of her bosom before lifting to her face. She was, without a doubt, one of the most beautiful females he'd ever encountered. All soft lines and ivory skin with hair just a shade lighter than the sun. The quintessential English rose. And she'd wanted to dance. With *him*. "When do you think that will be?"

"Hmmm?" She'd been looking at something – or someone – over his left shoulder, and it took her a moment to respond. "Oh, I'm not certain."

Evan's brow furrowed. "You're not certain when you'll return?"

"No." Was it his imagination, or had her demeanor suddenly cooled? "I'm sorry, Your Grace, but I fear my presence is requested on the other side of the room."

"Wait, I–" But she was already gone, the train of her ivory gown fluttering silently in her wake as she cut a path through the middle of the floor to where three other women stood waiting in front of a pillar, their expressions hidden behind large silk fans.

Giving a bemused shake of his head, Evan managed to hobble back to his corner. His champagne was exactly where he'd left it, and he drained what remained of the warm bubbly liquid in one swallow. For an instant he considered going after Lady Portia and asking for a second dance, but he didn't want to come on too strongly. Besides, he doubted his leg would hold up.

A glance at his gold pocket watch indicated the hour to be just shy of two in the morning, nearly fifteen minutes later than when he'd told his driver to be waiting for him outside. With one last cursory glance around the room – a vain attempt to make it appear as though he was looking at everyone when in fact he was really only looking for one person – he exited through a matching set of glass doors and onto a stone terrace that wrapped around the entire front of the house.

Standing at one end of the terrace was a bevy of females with their heads bent together. Evan clung to the shadows as he hobbled past them, only to stop short when his ears detected Lady Portia's sweet, melodious voice. Except it no longer sounded very sweet *or* melodious.

"Well, I did it." Her tone vaguely triumphant, Lady Portia opened her beaded reticule and held it out. "Five shillings each, if you please."

Evan frowned. What was she talking about?

"I cannot believe you let him *touch* you." With a visible shudder, a tall brunette standing to Lady Portia's left tossed a handful of coins into the reticule. "Weren't you afraid you were going to catch something?"

"He's not *diseased*, Nora." Lady Portia rolled her eyes. "He's disfigured. There's a difference."

"Not much of one." This from a slender redhead with a smattering of freckles across her nose. "What did he say to you?"

Lady Portia's snickering laugh cut through Evan like the sharpest of blades. "I haven't the faintest idea. I was concentrating too hard on not being sick to listen to a word he had to say. Honestly, I knew he was hideous, but up *close*..." She made a face. "It was horrible. I honestly don't know how the poor man gets out of bed every morning. He must keep every mirror in his house covered. It's such a pity he's a duke. All of that wealth and good breeding completely wasted."

Evan had heard more than enough. Unfortunately, when he tried to put weight down on his bad leg it buckled beneath him, even one dance having been too much for the fragile muscle and shattered bone. With a grunt and a curse he stumbled out of the shadows and fell down hard on his knees, drawing the attention of Lady Portia and her friends.

"Your Grace!" she gasped, and if not for what he'd just overheard Evan might have been tempted to believe her concern was genuine. "Are you all right? Here, let me help you."

"*Do not touch me*," he snarled when she crouched down beside him and reached for his arm. Her head canted to the side, the feigned worry sliding off her face as easily as dust being wiped off a table.

"Very well." Standing with the effortless grace of someone who'd never had their body betray them, Lady Portia watched Evan struggle to his feet with the faintest of smirks. When he was once again standing – more or less – she stepped out of his way and let him pass without speaking, her pitying stare saying more than words ever could.

Ashamed, angry, furiously betrayed, he gritted his teeth against the agonizing pain pulsing through his fractured limb and, through sheer will and determination, made it around the corner and down the steps before he collapsed against a stone wall covered in ivy, his tortured body refusing to take another step.

Never again, he vowed silently as he tilted his head back to glare bleakly up at the stars. He would never attend another ball. Never let himself be fooled by a beautiful woman. Never be stupid enough to believe anyone could see past the monster on the outside to the man beneath.

And, most importantly of all, he would never, ever fall in love.

Chapter One

"NOT *AGAIN*." Her nose wrinkling when she passed by her father's study and was overwhelmed by the unmistakable stench of cigar smoke and strong spirits, Hannah knocked softly on the door before letting herself in.

It took a moment for her eyes to adjust to the dim lighting. When they did, she was met with a familiar sight: Lord Fairchild slumped forward over his desk, one hand still wrapped around the bottle of brandy he'd used to drink himself into mindless oblivion and a cigar smoldering dangerously close to a towering stack of unpaid notes.

Hannah extinguished the cigar first and then dumped what remained of the brandy out the nearest window before tossing the empty bottle into a bin. Her father jolted when the glass clanged against metal, but with a snort and a loud snore he promptly fell back asleep.

“Oh Papa.” Tenderly covering his shoulders with a blanket before turning her attention to the various bank notes scattered across the desk, she began to sort through them one by one, the corners of her mouth tightening as she encountered one frivolous expense after another.

Honestly. Who needed *one* pair of crocodile skin gloves, let alone two? No wonder her poor father had tried to drown himself in brandy. Lord Fairchild was not the sort of man to idly indulge in spirits, but if there was one thing that made him reach for the bottle it was his wife and daughter’s penchant for spending beyond their means.

Lady Fairchild had never met a shiny bauble she didn’t like and her children, with the exception of Hannah, had all followed in her footsteps. Alice loved hats. Cadence adored reticules. And Sarah, it seemed, had recently developed a yearning for skinned reptiles.

For three weeks out of the month Lord Fairchild managed to turn a blind eye to his family’s outrageous spending, but on the fourth week – when notes were delivered in alarming quantities to their modest townhome on the outskirts of Berkeley Square – he locked himself in his study and scarcely emerged for days.

Hannah hadn’t the faintest idea how he had managed to keep the creditors at bay for this long, but she knew he wouldn't be able to keep it up much longer. Something which Lady Fairchild seemed incapable of understanding.

"*Eight* new dresses?" Staring at the note from Madame Dillard's in disbelief, Hannah was tempted to reach for the brandy herself. What were her sisters thinking? She'd told them time and again that they'd have to reuse their wardrobes from last season. A negligible sacrifice, given that every gown had been worn only once and some not at all.

Biting down on the tips of her fingers – a nervous habit she'd possessed since childhood – Hannah crossed to the window and let her forehead fall against the cool glass with a dull *thud*. There was no getting around it this time. They were going to find themselves in the poor house for sure, or – at the very least – be forced to strip the house bare and sell off everything that wasn't nailed down. Then re-wearing the same dress twice would be the *least* of her sister's concerns.

Without a shilling to their names, they'd quickly become the laughingstock of the *ton*. Something Cadence could ill afford now that she'd managed to capture the attention of an earl. And what would happen to Alice and Sarah, both of whom were so looking forward to their debuts? Born only three minutes apart, the twins had been counting down their launch into society since the day they could talk. Having it taken away would devastate them, not to mention the embarrassment of which would send Lady Fairchild into an early grave.

Something had to be done.

But what?

The most obvious answer was a marriage of means, but with Cadence all but promised to the Earl of Benfield (who, while well off, was by no stretch of the imagination wealthy enough to cover the Fairchild's outstanding debt) and the twins having yet to make their debut, that left Hannah.

Hannah, who had never met a man she was even remotely interested in marrying. Hannah, who – at the age of six and twenty – was perilously close to becoming a spinster. Hannah, who would rather attend a reading at the library than a fancy ball at Almack's. Hannah, who, after eight miserable seasons, had failed to attract a single suitor.

Lifting her head, she scowled at her reflection in the window. A young woman with gray eyes and thick chestnut hair pinned in a loose coil at the nape of her neck scowled back. Freckles dusted her nose and cheeks, giving her a youthful appearance that was countered by the generous swell of her bosom and the prominent curve of her backside. She had a wide mouth and a narrow chin, with a neck that was slightly too long and a body that lent itself to awkwardness.

A breathtaking swan Hannah was not – unlike her sisters, all of whom were strikingly beautiful – but she didn't mind her ordinary appearance. In fact, she rather liked it. When someone was *too* pretty they ran the risk of receiving attention that was less than genuine. Hannah, on the other hand, never had to worry if a gentleman was only paying attention to her because of her appearance.

Mostly because they never paid her any attention at all.

With an annoyed expulsion of breath she turned away from the window and left the study, leaving her father to sleep off the effects of his overindulgence until morning. After seeking out the housekeeper to ensure she would have a hot pot of coffee ready the moment Lord Fairfield awoke, she made her way up the creaking staircase to the bedroom she shared with Cadence. Alice and Sarah were across the way, and their parents had an adjoining chamber down the hall.

"Cadence, you're still awake," Hannah noted with some surprise as she tiptoed into the room and shut the door silently behind her. "I thought you'd gone to sleep ages ago."

Sitting in the middle of her bed with the blankets drawn up over her knees, Cadence set aside a well-worn copy of *Ackermann's Repository* and shrugged her shoulders. "I was waiting for you. How is Father?"

"How do you think he is?" Hannah said, her tone gently chiding. Not wanting to summon their lady's maid at such a late hour, she presented her back to Cadence and her sister automatically began to undo the long row of buttons that ran down the length of her dress. "We're lucky he hasn't taken what little money remains and run away to start a new life."

"He wouldn't do that." Cadence's hands stilled. "Would he?"

"No, of course not. Besides, there's no money to be had." She delivered a stern glare over her shoulder. "You spent it all on beaded reticules you didn't need."

"It wasn't *just* me," Cadence protested. "I *told* Sarah she didn't need two pairs of gloves, but she wouldn't listen."

"She never does," Hannah murmured as she shrugged out of her dress and carefully laid it over the back of a chair so as to avoid any unnecessary wrinkles. Whisking a long white nightgown over her head, she turned and regarded Cadence with a lifted brow. "It's serious this time. The creditors are going to be knocking on our door by the dozens, and there's nothing left to pay them with."

Her sister frowned. "There has to be *something* left. Father is a baron, for heaven's sake."

"A baron with three daughters and a wife who like to spend beyond their means," Hannah countered. "We should thank our stars if we're not homeless by the end of the month."

"I cannot be *homeless*," Cadence exclaimed, her eyes – several shades darker than Hannah's own and tip tilted at the corners to give her a feline appearance – widening in distress. "Where would I keep all of my dresses?"

Hannah bit her tongue.

Hard.

"When do you think Lord Benfield might present you with a proposal?" she asked after a long, heavy pause in which she struggled to rein in her exasperation. She knew her sister had only the best intentions, but just *once* she'd like for Cadence to take their financial predicament seriously. Heavens knew their mother and the twins weren't going to and their father, for all that he bellowed and blustered when the bills came due, never actually *did* anything about his family's atrocious spending. Which left Hannah and, to a lesser degree, Cadence, to pick up the pieces.

"I'd hope he might approach Father over the summer." A line of annoyance formed between Cadence's dark brows. "But he's dragging his heels."

A prickling of alarm swept down Hannah's spine as she sat on the edge of her bed. Lord Benfield may not have been able to pay off all their debts, but he could at least make a significant dent. But that was only if he did, in fact, marry Cadence. "Do you think he has changed his mind?"

"About marrying me? Of course not," said Cadence, looking insulted her sister would dare imply otherwise. "He has all but promised he will propose once his brother returns from his tour abroad."

"And when will that be?"

"At the end of the Season."

"At the end of the...but that's months away!" Hannah said, aghast.

Cadence pursed her lips. "So?"

"So we need a wealthy benefactor *now*, Cadence. Do you think Lord Benfield might help with some of our debts as a measure of good faith?" she asked hopefully. "You said yourself that you're practically engaged."

"I said no such thing," her sister said stiffly, "and I am not about to risk my proposal by demanding an allowance before we are even engaged. Everyone knows you wait until *after* you're married to spend their money."

"You don't have to demand. I'm sure if you asked nicely–"

Cadence's lips pinched together to form a hard, stubborn line. "No."

"But–"

"I said no, and that's the end of it. If we're in as dire straits as you say we are–"

"We are," Hannah interrupted.

"–then why don't *you* find an earl to marry? Or, better yet, a duke?"

"A duke?" Hannah was so startled by the suggestion she couldn't help but laugh. "Do be serious."

"I *am* being serious," Cadence insisted. "You do not give yourself enough credit, Han. If you put any effort at all into your appearance you're actually quite pretty-"

"Thank you," Hannah said dryly.

"–and you're far more intelligent than I am." Cadence frowned. "A bit *too* intelligent, actually. But that can be easily fixed. Our family doesn't have so much as a hint of scandal–"

"We're in debt up to our bonnets!"

"Yes, but no one else knows that." She paused. "Do they?"

Hannah shook her head. "Not that I know of, but it's only a matter of–"

"There, you see? You are an excellent candidate for a duchess."

"Because I am passably pretty, somewhat intelligent, and I haven't had an affair or otherwise besmirched the family name?"

Her sister smiled. It was a devious sort of smile, the kind a cat might wear right before it pounced on an unsuspecting bird. "Precisely. Now all we have to do is find you the right duke."

Chapter Two

Hannah hadn't the faintest idea if the notoriously reclusive Duke of Wycliffe was the right duke, but he was *a* duke, and she was desperate. Desperate enough to listen to Cadence's fool-brained idea. Desperate enough to hope it actually might work. Desperate enough to find herself in a hired hackney, gritting her teeth against every hard bump on the narrow, rocky road that led to Wycliffe Estate.

Sitting high on a hill overlooking hundreds of acres of dense wood and swampland, the aging manor house was a tired tribute to eras gone by with its cracked stone exterior, sagging roof, and dark, expressionless windows. The surrounding grounds were also in disrepair, the lawns untended and overgrown, the gardens filled with weeds, and the fountain in the middle of the drive overflowing with leaves and several inches of stagnant water.

Oh Cadence, Hannah thought in silent distress as the

hackney rolled to a stop amidst a cloud of dust. *What have you gotten me into* this *time?*

Her sister had been adamant that of all the eligible dukes in England, Wycliffe was the most likely to be receptive to Hannah's...*unusual*...proposal. But she'd failed to mention anything about the appalling condition of his estate, including how remote it was.

Instead, all she had said was that Wycliffe was an eligible bachelor who had suffered a grave injury as a child and as a result had spent much of his adulthood in seclusion. When Hannah had asked for more details she'd merely shrugged and said, *'He is not married and he's a duke. What else is there to know?'*

Hannah vaguely recalled overhearing a rumor about Wycliffe a few seasons back, but having never been one to pay attention to gossip it had gone in one ear and out the other. Now, as the driver came around the side of the hackney and opened the door, she wished she had paid closer attention.

"Wait." Elsbeth, her lady's maid – and the only person aside from Cadence who knew that she wasn't *really* visiting Great Aunt Martha in Surrey – placed a restraining hand on Hannah's arm when she started to stand up. "Are you sure this is a good idea?"

Hannah smiled wryly at her maid, a tiny slip of a thing whose blonde hair and blue eyes revealed her German ancestry. "I'm not sure of anything, except that if this doesn't work you are soon to be without a job and my father will be sent to debtor's prison."

"But what will happen if he turns us away?" Elsbeth fretted.

"Truth be told, I am more afraid of what will happen if he *doesn't*." With a strained smile that was as much for her own benefit as the maid's, Hannah stepped down from the hackney and squared her shoulders.

It had taken them two full days and half of another to reach the duke's isolated estate and the sun was already heavy in the sky, touching everything with a golden glow that helped to soften the manor's harsh lines and crumbling edges.

With a bit of imagination it wasn't hard to picture what the grand old house must have looked like before time and neglect had taken their toll, and Hannah couldn't help but wonder if the duke was in a similar state of dishevelment. She supposed at this point there was nothing else to do but find out for herself.

Holding fast to what little courage she still possessed after traveling halfway across England on some of the most treacherous roads she'd ever had the misfortune of encountering, Hannah walked up to the front door, raised her gloved hand – which, despite the thunderous beat of her heart, was impressively steady – and knocked.

When there was no response, she bit the inside of her cheek and knocked again.

"Perhaps the butler is off today?" Elsbeth suggested, although she didn't sound very convinced. "Or maybe the duke is not in residence. We should return home."

Hannah frowned at the maid over her shoulder. "We are not going anywhere," she said firmly. "And we certainly did not come all this way just to return home before I even *meet* him. Chin up, Elsbeth. No harm will befall us."

"That's precisely what people say right before harm *does* befall them," Elsbeth muttered under her breath. She visibly jumped when the hackney suddenly pulled away, and Hannah couldn't help but feel a twinge of apprehension deep in her gut as she watched the team of matching grays trot off down the drive.

There was no turning back now. Not with the nearest inn a full day's walk and nightfall rapidly approaching. Turning back towards the door, she knocked with renewed vigor. "I am sure there is a perfectly good explanation as to why no one...*oh*," she gasped as the door was abruptly yanked open to reveal a man standing on the other side of it, his towering frame draped in shadow and his mouth curled in a sneer.

"What do you want?" he growled, his voice as rough as the roads they'd travelled to get here.

"I…" As her carefully crafted speech – the one she'd spent the past two days rehearsing over and over again until every word was burned into her mind – vanished in a puff of proverbial smoke, Hannah could only gape at the stranger in stunned silence. And pray, as she'd never prayed before, that he was the butler. Or the footman. Or even the cook. Anyone, *anyone*, but the Duke of Wycliffe. "I…"

"Are you deaf?" he said, black eyes glittering with thinly veiled fury as his gaze swept across her. "I asked you a question and I expect an answer. *What do you want?*"

Elsbeth squeaked and scurried to the edge of the fountain.

Coward, Hannah thought silently.

The man started to shut the door. Without thinking, Hannah stuck her foot out.

"Wait!" she cried. "I – I should very much like to speak to the Duke of Wycliffe."

His black eyes narrowed. "There's no duke here."

"Are – are you certain?" Her gaze slid to the gold buttons on his waistcoat. "Because–"

"I'm positive," he snapped and Hannah barely had time to yank her worn ankle boot out of the way before he slammed the door with so much force the windows rattled. Jaw sagging, she stared at the door in stunned disbelief. Was *that* whom she'd come all this way to marry? If so, Cadence had quite a bit of explaining to do!

"Well you heard him," Elsbeth piped up. "The duke isn't in. If we leave now, maybe we could catch up with the hackney."

"Elsbeth, that *was* the duke." Raising her fist, Hannah began to pummel the door with renewed vigor, unable to believe anyone – least of all a duke! – could be so unforgivably rude. "Excuse me!" she called out, raising her voice to a near shout. "Excuse me, but I was not done speaking. If you would be so kind as to open the door–"

"Will you *stop* that incessant pounding? You're giving me a bloody headache." Yanking the door open, the duke glared down at Hannah. Fisting her hands on her hips, Hannah glared up at the duke. When it became clear that neither one was willing to back down, Wycliffe muttered something indecipherable under his breath and stepped out into the muted sunlight.

"Who are you?" he demanded, folding his arms across his chest. Tall and rangy, he towered over her by at least six inches, forcing her to tilt her head all the way back in order to look him in the eye.

"Who are *you*?" she countered. "I've come to speak to the Duke of Wycliffe, and–"

"You're speaking to him." A muscle ticked in his jaw, inadvertently drawing her gaze to a large puckered knot of flesh on the right side of his face. She hadn't seen the scar before when he'd been standing in the shadows. Stark white against his golden complexion, it began at the top of his ear and extended all the way down to the edge of his chin. Seeing the direction of her stare, the duke's expression grew shuttered. "Should I bend down so you can get a closer look?" he said caustically.

"No. No, I…" Finding herself at a loss of words, she bit her lip. "I am sorry."

"Don't be." His shoulder jerked, shrugging away the scar as it were nothing more than a papercut instead of something that must have caused him immense physical and emotional pain. "It happened a long time ago."

"Does it still hurt?" she asked without thinking.

Looking slightly taken aback at the personal question, the duke frowned and gave a curt shake of his head. A wavy lock of hair as black as his eyes tumbled over his brow and he pushed it aside with an impatient flick of his wrist. "No. It doesn't."

"That – that's good." He had strong features, Hannah noted. Not handsome. The angles of his cheekbones and the prominent cut of his nose were far too sharp to be handsome. Then there was the scar to contend with. But what was beauty, if not imperfect?

"What do you want?" He shifted his weight from one leg to the other. A grimace passed over his countenance as though the small movement had caused him discomfort, but his fierce gaze never wavered. "I will not ask again."

"I…" Her chest rose and fell beneath the heavy fabric of her traveling habit as she took a deep, bracing breath. "I have a – a proposal for you."

"A proposal?" Thick brows gathered over the bridge of his nose. "What sort of proposal?"

There was a part of Hannah that wanted to turn around and run all the way back to London. To jump into bed and pull the covers over her head and pretend everything was going to magically sort itself out. After all, *she* hadn't been running willy-nilly around town buying everything that caught her eye, nor had she been ignoring their mounting debt hoping it would simply disappear. Her parents were responsible for the mess they found themselves in. A mess they both still refused to acknowledge, as if it really *was* going to go away on its own.

Someone had to do something. And that someone, it seemed, was her.

Whether she liked it or not.

Not, Hannah thought silently as she eyed the duke. Definitely not. Wycliffe wasn't at all like Cadence had painted him to be: a lonely, somewhat awkward bachelor who preferred the company of books to people.

That duke she could relate to. *That* duke she had something in common with. But *this* duke, with his flashing eyes and contemptuous sneer, was – to put it mildly – quite out of her league.

"Well?" he growled. "Out with it."

Hannah blinked. "I...er...well…"

She thought of when she was a young girl and she'd accidentally knocked over one of her mother's beloved Davenport vases. In her haste to pick up the broken pieces she'd cut herself on the palm of her hand. Not wanting to tell her mother what had happened, she'd invoked Cadence's help in wrapping the wound. All had gone well...until she'd attempted to remove the bandage later that day only to discover it had adhered itself to the cut.

Inch by excruciating inch she'd pried the fabric back, until Cadence – with her usual aplomb – had marched up, grabbed hold of the bandage, and yanked the entire thing off in one fell swoop.

How it had hurt! The sting had been like a hundred tiny hornets attacking her palm at once. But as quickly as the pain appeared it faded away, and Hannah had learned a valuable lesson: sometimes you just needed to rip the bandage off.

"My proposal is an actual proposal." Lifting her chin, she stared steadily into the cold, fathomless depths of the duke's menacing gaze. "My name is Miss Hannah Fairchild, and I should very much like to marry you."

Chapter Three

IF EVAN DIDN'T think the girl was completely daft before, he did now.

He stared at her in astonishment, searching in vain for some sign that she was jesting with him. A twinkle in those arresting gray eyes. A tiny smirk curling the corner of that delectable pink mouth. Instead he saw nothing but quiet sincerity which was how he knew she was dicked in the nob. Although she didn't *look* crazy. Truth be told, she looked...well, she looked rather beautiful in a disheveled sort of way, like a wildflower that had accidentally been placed in the middle of an elegant bouquet of roses.

Her clothes were dusty and travel worn, her hat scrunched up on one side as if she'd accidentally sat on it. Her hair, the same color as the leaves still clinging to the branches of the large red maple at the end of the drive, had come partially undone from its chignon and framed the sides of her face in a tangled spill of auburn silk. A dusting of freckles and a nose that was ever-so-slightly off center kept her from true beauty. That, and the smudge of purple – jam, perhaps? – on the edge of her chin.

The muscles in Evan's abdomen inadvertently tightened as he imagined drawing Miss Hannah Fairchild in close, lowering his head, and licking that little spot of sticky sweetness away. Then his eyes narrowed, and his shoulders drew back, and he looked at her with renewed suspicion as an unpleasant thought suddenly dampened his ardor.

"Colebrook put you up to this, didn't he? Bastard," Evan cursed under his breath. A neighboring landowner, the Duke of Colebrook enjoyed fast horses, loose women, and being a general pain in the arse. He was supposed to be in London, but Evan wouldn't put it past him to have arranged for a little parting gift before he left. Colebrook did love his pranks, and he never passed up an opportunity to get under Evan's skin.

Two weeks ago he'd been woken in the middle of the night by a trio of drunken sailors singing in the foyer. How Colebrook had managed that small feat he hadn't the bloodiest idea, as the nearest port was a good fifty miles away. It had taken him the better part of an hour and his second best bottle of brandy to coax them out of the house.

Then there'd been the time Colebrook had replaced all of the horses in his barn with milking goats. Compared to that, hiring a woman to show up on his doorstep and propose marriage was child's play. But judging by the puzzlement on Hannah's face she was either a very good actress or she had absolutely no idea who Evan was talking about.

"Colebrook?" She bit down on her bottom lip. "I – I am afraid I don't know a Mr. Colebrook."

"Never mind," Evan said curtly. His gaze shifted to the dark-haired woman standing by the fountain. She was staring intently at the ground, her stiff posture indicating she'd rather be anywhere else than where she currently was.

That made two of them.

"Your traveling companion, I presume?" he asked.

"My lady's maid, yes. Your Grace–"

"Where is your carriage?" he interrupted.

Gray eyes peeked up at him beneath a thick curtain of dark red lashes. "I – I sent it away."

"You sent it away?" Evan stared down at her incredulously. "Why the devil would you do that? Have you any idea how far you are from the nearest village?"

"I do, yes, but–"

“I suppose you thought you’d just avail yourself of my carriage and driver, did you?” His leg was beginning to ache from standing so long in one spot, but he clenched his jaw and pushed the pain to the back of his mind. “I am sorry to say my driver is indisposed at the moment.” A tiny white lie to cover up the fact that he’d let the man go months ago, having no reason to employ him given that he never left the estate.

“I did not travel all this way just to use your carriage and driver, Your Grace.” The corners of Hannah’s mouth tucked into a frown. “That would be absurd.”

Evan’s eyebrows shot up. “Oh *that* would be absurd, would it? But I suppose arriving unannounced on a stranger’s doorstep and proposing marriage is perfectly normal?”

“It’s not as farfetched as you make it seem. If you would just let me explain–”

“No.”

Her hands unfolding from her chest to settle on her hips, Hannah lifted her chin and scowled up at him. “Has anyone ever told you how rude it is to interrupt someone when they’re speaking?”

“Has anyone ever told you how rude it is to show up uninvited?” he countered.

“I told you, if you would let me–”

“Let you explain. Yes, I heard you the first time.” And

though he was loathe to admit it out loud, part of him wanted very much to hear that explanation. Almost as much as he wanted to kiss that impertinent little mouth. Evan's brow furrowed. Where had *that* thought come from? Yes, the chit was pleasing to look at, but there was also the distinct possibility that she was completely insane and the last thing he wanted – the last thing he *needed* – was a troublesome female in his life. Troublesome females were the reason he'd left London in the first place. And yet…

"Are you certain Colebrook did not send you?"

"No one sent me. I came of my own accord."

"To propose marriage."

"Yes," she said without hesitation. "Precisely."

He studied her for a long moment, his gaze lingering on the jam that still clung to the edge of her chin before jerking back up to meet her eyes. They were the soft gray of a sky after a heavy rain; that quiet moment of solace between the storm and the sunshine. He'd never seen a shade quite like it before. "All right, Miss Fairchild." Stepping stiffly to the side, he gestured her into the dimly lit foyer with a mocking sweep of his arm. "Let's hear this explanation of yours."

FINALLY, HANNAH THOUGHT as she walked past Wycliffe. She'd started to fear he was going to leave her standing on the doorstep all night. Although truthfully she didn't know which was worse: being left to face the elements or strolling blindly into the proverbial lion's den.

She supposed she was about to find out.

"Please, have a seat." The duke led her into an adjoining parlor and nodded towards a velvet chaise lounge that looked as though it hadn't been used for a very long time. Her suspicions were confirmed when she sat down and a plume of dust flew up, causing her to sneeze.

"I do not get many visitors," Wycliffe said as he sat across from her in a high backed wooden chair. Elsbeth remained discreetly in the hallway, having declined Hannah's invitation to join them in the parlor.

"I cannot imagine why," Hannah muttered, her stomach rolling queasily when she spied what looked like mouse droppings on the armrest. Creditors or no creditors, if a rodent dashed across the floor she was leaving. Having been bitten by a rat as a young child, she positively loathed anything with whiskers and a long skinny tail.

"What was that?" Wycliffe asked.

"Nothing," she said quickly. Glancing around the room, she discovered it to be in the same sad state of neglect as the exterior of the manor. The curtains were dark and dingy, the floorboards were badly in need of a polish, and the furniture– what there was of it – was covered in a thick coating of dust.

"Is your housekeeper indisposed as well?" she couldn't help but ask.

"No." He followed her gaze to the dormant fireplace which was overflowing with soot. "As I said, I do not get many visitors. Which begs the question as to why *you* are here."

"Yes." She cleared her throat. "About that…"

"I am waiting, Miss Fairchild." He drummed his fingers on the slender armrests of his chair. "Albeit not very patiently."

"As I said when I first arrived I have, ah, a proposal." What to do with her hands, Hannah wondered? She'd never had a problem with them before, but now they did not want to sit quietly on her lap, nor did she dare put them on the lounge. As a result they fluttered restlessly in midair, fingers curling and uncurling as she desperately tried to act natural. Or at least as natural as one could act while sitting across from a duke with the demeanor of an angry bear.

An angry bear who has just been roused from his den and poked with a sharp stick, she added silently when Wycliffe's eyebrows lowered and his mouth tightened, pulling his scar taut.

"I believe we've established that, Miss Fairchild. The

question is no longer *what* you are doing here, but *why* you are here. What could have possibly possessed you to travel untold miles across some of the worst roads England has to offer in hopes of marrying a man you've never met?"

"I am not crazy," she said defensively, not liking his tone or what it implied. "I have a very good reason for being there."

"And that reason is?" he drawled when she fell silent.

"I need a wealthy husband, Your Grace." She hadn't intended to be so blunt, but Wycliffe seemed like the sort of man who would appreciate candor. "And if the state of your household is any indication, you are badly in need of a wife."

"What does my household have to do with anything?" he scowled.

"Nothing. It's just that…well…" Her gaze flicked to a large vertical crack in the plaster wall behind Wycliffe's head. "Everything's falling apart a little bit, isn't it? And – and I hate to be the one to tell you, but I believe you may have a rodent infestation."

"So I'll get a cat," he said with a negligent shrug. "Why the devil do I need a wife?"

"Someone to help organize your personal affairs?" she suggested.

"That's what my valet is for."

"Someone to entertain guests?"

"I told you." Those dark eyes peered into hers with such intensity she wondered if he wasn't gazing into her very soul. "I do not receive many guests."

"Maybe you'd get more if there weren't mouse droppings on your furniture." She looked meaningfully down at her armrest. When he simply stared at her she cleared her throat and said, "What about companionship?"

"I'll get two cats."

Hannah huffed out an exasperated breath. Her sister had said the duke was a tad eccentric, but she'd failed to mention he was stubborn as a mule. At least now she understood why some men dragged their heels at proposing marriage. It was embarrassing, to be turned down. Particularly when your only competition was a *cat*.

But she couldn't give up.

She wouldn't.

Not when her family was depending on her persistence.

Sitting up as straight as her spine would allow, she frowned at Wycliffe and adopted her best, most businesslike tone. The same tone she employed when the twins needed to be put in their place, or Cadence needed to be told that no, she couldn't buy three pairs of the same exact shoe just in case one pair got muddy.

"Your Grace, I would not be here if my circumstances were anything less than dire. You see, my father is struggling to keep up with creditors and–"

"So you want money," Wycliffe cut in. The corners of his mouth curled in a derisive sneer. "I should have thought as much."

"No," Hannah corrected him sharply. "I want a husband. I am not a beggar and I am not looking for a handout. I am a woman of marriageable age and impeccable social standing who does not have the luxury of time. If I did, you can rest assured that I would not be here asking a complete stranger to marry me."

The duke's chair gave an ominous creak as he leaned back and canted his head to the side. "No other man would have you, would they?"

Hannah shifted uncomfortably on the chaise lounge. "You could say that I've been very…selective."

Wycliffe didn't bother to disguise his snort. "And I just so happen to fit the bill, do I? Since this is the first time we've met, let me tell you a little about myself, Miss Fairchild. I'm a bastard," he said flatly. "Perhaps not in the literal since, but every other possible way. I live all the way out here for one reason and one reason only: I dislike people, women in particular. I am often rude, callous, and insensitive. Then there is my physical impairment, which I am sure you have noticed." His jaw hardened. “Suffice it to say, I am not husband material. You have wasted your time, Miss Fairchild. Worst yet, you’ve wasted mine.”

“I don’t think I have,” Hannah said softly.

“Oh really?” he asked, the bite of sarcasm in his voice unmistakable. “And how is that?”

She glanced down at her lap. “You’re correct. You are rude, callous, and insensitive. Not to mention boorish, arrogant, and unkind. As for your physical impairment, well, none of us are perfect, are we?” She looked up. “I am not seeking perfection, Your Grace. I have flaws, although admittedly not as many as you.” Her mouth creased in the tiniest of smiles which Wycliffe did not return. He watched her intently, his expression unreadable save a faint tick in the corner of his jaw.

“Go on,” he said.

“What I want – what I need – is a husband who will settle my father’s debts. In return, I will not interfere with your life or how you wish to live it. I will care for your household, such as it is, and turn visitors away, if that’s what you want. I will make no requests of you, nor ask you to change in any way.”

“I already live my life how I want to *without* a wife.” One dark brow lifted. “What makes you think I wish to complicate matters by acquiring one?”

“What about an heir?” Hannah’s cheeks suffused with

color. She was loathe to discuss such an intimate subject, but Wycliffe had left her no choice. "Surely you wish to have a child. A son to inherit your lands and title. That will be impossible without a wife."

A flicker of emotion – Surprise? Curiosity? Annoyance? It was impossible to tell – passed over his countenance. "I'm thirty, not eighty. I've time yet to sire offspring, if I ever have such an inclination."

"But what about a wife?" she pressed. "You would need to be married for any child to be considered legitimate."

"Miss Fairchild." His tone held a hint of amusement. "I had no idea you were so forward."

"I am determined," she corrected. "And intelligent enough to realize a perfect opportunity when I see one. Men and women have married for far less sustainable reasons than the one's I have just presented, Your Grace. Please say you'll at least consider my proposal."

"And if I refuse?" he said coolly.

"Then I will find someone who will." It was a complete bluff. The Duke of Wycliffe was her last hope. Having eight failed seasons behind her, she wasn't foolish enough to believe the ninth one would be the charm. If this didn't work, her family was going to find themselves in the poorhouse for sure. She gritted her teeth. "Your Grace–"

“I will do it.” He spoke it so abruptly that at first she was certain she’d misunderstood him.

“You’ll…do what?”

“Marry you. I will marry you, Miss Fairchild.” His eyes narrowed. “Isn’t that what you wanted? Isn’t that what you came all the bloody way out here for?”

“Yes. It is. But…just like that? You’ll marry me just like that?”

“Just like that,” he confirmed with a curt inclination of his chin. “I presume you’d rather the nuptials occur sooner rather than later?”

“Ah, yes. Yes, the sooner the better. My father–”

“I will ensure any outstanding credits in his name will be paid in full by the end of the week.”

Her mouth opened. Closed. “But – but I haven’t told you the amount yet,” she said faintly.

“The amount is of no consequence. I only ask that he show some financial restraint in the future.” Wycliffe’s eyes bored into hers. “I am an extremely wealthy man, Miss Fairchild, but I abhor frivolous spending.”

At least we have one thing in common, Hannah thought silently.

“It’s getting late, and you are no doubt weary from your travels.” Favoring his right leg ever-so-slightly, Wycliffe stood up. “I will have a maid show you to one of the guest bedrooms.”

"One without mice, I hope," she quipped.

The duke's mouth twisted in a humorless smile. "The mice are the least of your concerns, Miss Fairchild."

And on that ominous note, he limped out of the parlor.

Chapter Four

Evan woke at dawn the next morning after a night spent tossing and turning and regretting his decision to accept Miss Hannah Fairchild's outrageous proposal. Unfortunately, there was no going back now. He may have been a bastard, but he was a bastard who stood by his word. Which meant for better or worse – in this case, almost certainly worse – he was soon to be a married man. To a woman he knew absolutely nothing about.

That's not completely true, he mused as he rolled out of bed and immediately sank into the hot bath he had his valet draw for him at the start of each day. As the chamomile-infused water lapped over his aching muscles he rested his head on the edge of the porcelain tub and stared up at the ceiling.

He knew the color of Hannah's eyes. Soft gray, like the fur of a rabbit.

He knew the shape of her smile, although he would have liked to see it without the brackets of tension framing the corners of her mouth.

He knew the curves of her body. Shapely and plump, like a golden pear ripe for the picking.

And he knew she was brave, as only a brave woman – or an incredibly stupid one – would dare ask a duke to marry her. But what was courage, he reflected as he stood up and walked naked across his bedchamber, if not stupidity in the face of the impossible?

"Breeches or trousers today, Your Grace?" Entering the room after a courteous knock, Evan's valet, a forty-something year old man of medium height and build, went to the large armoire in the corner of the room and held up one of each. After a moment's consideration, Evan nodded at the pair of tan trousers.

"I will not be riding this morning, Peterson. I have other matters to attend to."

"Would these matters having anything to do with our two guests sleeping in the west wing?" Peterson waited until Evan had put on the clothes he'd selected and sat down in a chair facing the window before he approached him with a straight razor. His movements well practiced and precise, he shaved his employer's chin and jaw with quick flicks of his wrist while Evan stared straight ahead.

"The guests to whom you are referring are Miss

Hannah Fairchild and her maid." When he'd woken the sky had been dark and gray, the clouds heavy and saturated with rain. After a light drizzle they'd begun to disperse, revealing a clear blue sky and the promise of a cool, crisp autumn day. "They will be staying with us."

Peterson paused with the razor angled along the side of Evan's throat. "Might I inquire as to how long?"

"Indefinitely, I suppose. Miss Fairchild and I are engaged."

For the first time in all the years Peterson had been serving Evan, first as a livery boy and then as a footman and finally as his own personal valet, his hand slipped and Evan hissed out a breath when he felt the sharp edge of the blade slice into his flesh. Gingerly touching his jaw, he regarded Peterson with a lifted brow when his fingertips came away covered in blood.

"I think I've quite enough scars, don't you?"

"I - I'm terribly sorry, Your Grace," the valet stuttered, his entire face turning as red as the apples weighing down the trees in the back orchards. "It was an accident. I – I don't know what happened. Please forgive me."

Evan brushed off the apology. He had more pressing matters to attend to than scolding his valet for one small mistake. "My waistcoat, if you would. I need to go speak with my bride-to-be."

HANNAH LOOKED UP when she saw a flicker of movement at the top of the stairs. Coming to a halt in the middle of the foyer, she watched without moving as the Duke of Wycliffe – and her future husband, although she'd yet to fully believe it – made his way down the steps.

He descended the master staircase with the rigidity of someone who had to consider each individual footfall. There was not a limp in his gait per say, but there was certainly a stiffness. She assumed the injury had come from his accident as a young child and she yearned to ask him what had happened. Not out of morbid curiosity, but to try to better understand the man who would soon be her husband. One glance at his furrowed brow, however, and she knew any questions about his past would have to wait.

"Good morning!" she said, her voice filled with a sunny optimism she didn't quite feel. How could she? Wycliffe may have agreed to her proposal, but at the end of the day she was still marrying a complete stranger. One who scowled more than he smiled and didn't seem at all keen to marry her, even though he'd agreed – for reasons that remained a mystery – to do precisely that.

"Walk with me," he said curtly.

"Walk – walk with you where?" Bewildered by the odd request, she nonetheless fell into step beside him as he marched out the front door and across the overgrown lawn. Weeds, still damp with morning dew, slapped against Hannah's skirts as she struggled to keep up. For a man with a physical impairment, the duke certainly kept a brisk pace.

"Where are we going?" Huffing a bit – it was no secret she preferred eating to exercise – Hannah failed to notice Wycliffe had suddenly stopped until it was too late. With a gasp and a soft cry she slammed into his back, the force of her momentum sending them both tumbling down a short embankment to land in a thicket of late blooming goldenrod.

The duke twisted as he fell, his strong arms wrapping around Hannah's smaller body in a vicelike grip that held her anchored against his chest even after their reckless descent had reached its conclusion. For a few precious seconds neither one of them moved and the only sounds came from the thunderous crash of the duke's heart beating against her breast and the quiet rustling of the goldenrod as it swayed in the wind.

"Are you injured?" Wycliffe asked. Keeping one arm secured around her waist he used the other to prop himself up on his elbow so he could look down at her, his gaze every bit as formidable as it had been in the parlor save the tiniest, *tiniest* glimmer of concern.

Or perhaps it was just a fleck of goldenrod.

"Just my pride." Her attempted smile emerging as

more of a grimace, Hannah struggled to push herself into a sitting position. A rather difficult maneuver, given that she was still pinned against the duke's chest. The duke's very hard, very *muscular* chest.

From everything Cadence had told her about him she'd imagined a weak invalid who rarely ventured outside the library, but it was clear – in more ways than one – that Wycliffe was neither weak nor an invalid. No, her husband-to-be was very much a man. A powerful, attractive–

"Good. Maybe next time you'll pay better attention."

–infuriating man.

"I shall strive to do my best," she said, tucking a strand of hair behind her ear. Wycliffe frowned down at her suspiciously, no doubt wondering if she was being sincere or mocking him. Hannah wondered the same thing herself. "Would you mind allowing me to get up?" Uncomfortably aware of just how intimate their current position was, she tried once again to free herself from Wycliffe's embrace, but like a wire snare the arm around her waist only tightened.

"I don't like clumsy women," he growled.

"And I don't like rude, overbearing dukes," she retorted.

They glared at each other as they'd done in the doorway except this time neither one showed any signs of backing down. Hannah couldn't say how long they laid there in the goldenrod, but it was long enough for her to notice the shallow cut on the side of his neck. Long enough for her to realize his eyes weren't black, as she'd initially thought, but a deep, deep midnight blue. Long enough for her to wonder what his mouth would taste like.

Those blue eyes abruptly darkened as he followed the direction of her gaze, her only warning before his hand curled possessively around the nape of her neck and he claimed her lips in a drugging kiss that was nothing like she'd expected…and everything she'd secretly yearned for.

Unlike the heroines in some of her favorite books, Hannah had never been kissed in the moonlight or in a gazebo. She'd never been pinned up against a brick wall or pushed into a lilac bush (the latter of which sounded rather painful, but who was she to judge?). As the seasons ticked by one after another she began to wonder if she would *ever* be kissed…and by whom. Thankfully she did not have to wonder any longer.

Wycliffe's kiss was as contradictory as the man himself. At turns soft and hard, then demanding and coaxing, he stole the breath from her lungs and the heart from her chest in long shallow sips that left her yearning for more.

Heat pooled low in her belly as he deepened the kiss, his tongue tracing the seam of her lips before sweeping boldly inside. The hand at her nape moved down, fingers tracing the delicate bumps of her vertebrae through the thin fabric of her dress until his palm cupped her hip. He squeezed and she squirmed, instinctively – albeit tentatively – rubbing herself against the hardest part of his body.

His savage growl stopped her short. Fearing she'd done something wrong, she peered up at him through her lashes, gray eyes wide and uncertain.

"I'm sorry," she whispered. "Have I hurt–"

"Do it again," he rasped, and so she did. Again and again as he continued to kiss her until the fire between them was raging so hot and so high it was a small miracle the meadow did not spontaneously ignite.

He touched her breasts, the rough pad of his thumb scraping over her nipples until she was panting from the pleasure of it. They rolled across the grass, flattening sprigs of goldenrod beneath them as their kiss deepened into something far more wicked than the innocent brush of lips upon lips.

Wycliffe blazed a scorching trail up her leg as he slipped his hand beneath her skirts and explored the creamy plumpness of her thigh. Hannah stiffened when she felt the gentle weight of his palm pressing against her curls, then softened like honey melting into a warm cup of tea when he began to use his fingers in a most extraordinary way.

"Oh," she whispered dazedly. "That's…that's quite nice."

He growled something indecipherable before he captured her mouth with his, drawing her bottom lip between his teeth and biting down with just enough pressure to elicit a gasp. He soothed the small bite with a flick of his tongue at the same time his finger slipped inside of her and Hannah was lost.

Head flung back, eyes heavy with passion, body drunk with desire, she opened herself to pleasure she'd never dreamed possible. Like the most skilled of musicians, Wycliffe strummed her core as if she were a finely tuned instrument until every inch of her was quivering in anticipation. Anticipation of what, precisely, she couldn't be certain…until all of a sudden everything tightened and held and then with a single stroke of his finger it came crashing down in wave after wave of mind-numbing bliss.

When the last wave had finally ebbed, Hannah opened her eyes and sat up on her elbows to discover her betrothed sitting a few feet away with his back facing her, shoulders rigid beneath the sharp line of his jacket. She bit her swollen lip, wanting to say something…anything, really, to break the awkward silence that had fallen between them. But just what *did* one say to a man who had been a stranger two days ago, a fiancé yesterday, and today – well, she didn't know what he was today.

"I apologize," Wycliffe said without looking at her. "That should not have happened."

"It's all right," Hannah said, for surely something that had felt so wonderful couldn't possibly be wrong. Mayhap in the eyes of God since they were not yet technically husband and wife, but given they were engaged He couldn't be *that* displeased with her. Lust may have been one of the seven deadly sins, but surely it paled in comparison to gluttony, greed, and wrath. Unfortunately, Wycliffe did not seem to be on the same mindset.

"No," he said flatly, "it's not. And it will not happen again."

A flicker of panic unfurled in Hannah's chest when he stood up. Pushing down her skirts, she hastened to do the same. "What do you mean? Are we – that is to say, have you…"

"Called off the wedding?" Dark gaze unreadable, he turned to face her. "No. As I said, Miss Fairchild, I am a man of my word."

Her lips curved in a hesitant smile. "Given what just happened, I – I think we can use our Christian names.

Don't you?"

"I do not. You may refer to me as Your Grace or Wycliffe, I have no preference. And I shall continue to call you Miss Fairchild."

"Even after we're married?" she asked, her brow furrowing.

"*Especially* after we are married."

A loose coil of hair tumbled into Hannah's eyes as she shook her head in bewilderment. "I am afraid I do not understand."

"It's quite simple, really." His gaze flicked to the flattened section of goldenrod before returning to her face. For an instant his countenance seemed to soften…and then his jaw clenched and his emotions were once again hidden behind an impenetrable wall of ice and stone. "This marriage is not a love match, Miss Fairchild. It is a means of convenience. A business transaction, if you will, in which both parties benefit equally. There is no reason to bring love into it, or intimacy for that matter. If the time comes that I desire an heir, I shall make the necessary arrangements. Until then, you need not fear I will come knocking at your door in the middle of the night."

How *clinical* he made it all sound. Frowning, Hannah tucked her hair behind her ear. Maybe she should have been grateful that Wycliffe was all but insisting their marriage be in name only. And a tiny part of her was. But a much bigger part – the part that had just been rolling about in wanton abandon – wanted more. “What if we come to care for one another in time?”

“We won’t.”

“But if we did,” she persisted, “what would be the harm?”

“The harm?” he repeated, looking down at her as if she’d just suggested the earth was flat or the sun was green. “The harm is that love is for fools, Miss Fairchild. And while I may be many things, a fool is not one of them.”

But as the duke walked away, Hannah couldn’t help but think that someone who did not believe in love was the biggest fool of them all.

Chapter Five

They were married two weeks later on a rainy autumn day with only the priest, Elsbeth, and Peterson in attendance. Hannah had written to her family to tell them of her engagement, and while they were thrilled for her – Cadence in particular – they'd been unable to make the long journey due to the Season having just begun.

While she did wish her parents could have been there to see her married, Hannah was equally glad they had remained in London as the entire ceremony lasted less than ten minutes. There had been the reading of the vows, a few readings from the bible, one chaste kiss on her cheek, and then it was over. In the blink of an eye – or so it seemed – she was the new Duchess of Wycliffe. Although truth be told she neither felt like a bride *or* a duchess.

After the wedding, which had taken place in a small

church on the outskirts of the nearest village, she and Wycliffe returned to the estate where he promptly disembarked from their carriage and retreated into his study.

For the next several days the only time Hannah saw her husband was when they dined together in the evenings. Even then there was little conversation as it was rather difficult to converse with someone when separated by a fifteen foot table, although she did try. Unfortunately, all of her efforts were rebuked and after it became clear that the duke was more interested in his soup than his duchess, she stopped trying.

After dinner Wycliffe usually went on a walk and Hannah went to her bedchamber where she pretended everything was going to be all right.

Every marriage started off a bit rocky at first, she told herself as she worked on her embroidery or tried to read a book. Particularly ones where the bride and groom were veritable strangers. Wycliffe would come around eventually. Their marriage might not have started off as a love match, but that didn't mean it couldn't become one with a little time and understanding…no matter *what* her husband had said to the contrary.

Where there was passion, Hannah reasoned, there could be love. And there had been plenty of passion to be found in their kiss. Wycliffe's words may have said one thing, but his body – and the dark desire in his eyes as he'd pinned her to the ground – had said quite another.

He wanted her. She was sure of it. He just didn't *want* to want her.

And therein laid the problem.

Hannah would be the first to admit that when she first set off for Wycliffe Manor love was the furthest thing from her mind. She wanted first and foremost to save her family. Everything else was secondary. Then she'd met the duke…and then he'd kissed her…and suddenly love hadn't felt secondary at all.

But what to do? Better yet, how to do it? *That*, Hannah decided as she wandered aimlessly around the manor on a self-guided tour of her new home, *was the question.*

Rain pattered against the windows as she walked through the library, a parlor with all of the furniture covered beneath large white sheets, and a drawing room without any furniture at all. Everything was buried underneath a thick layer of dust and there were heavy drapes on all of the windows. The drapes, combined with the flickering candlelight and pitter patter of rain on the glass, gave the manor a dark, grim tone that lifted the tiny hairs on the back of her neck as she walked from one room to the next. Yet the manor wasn't completely hopeless. Beneath the dirt and behind the shadows was a house with good bones just waiting to be brought back to life. Removing those awful drapes, polishing the woodwork with a bit of beeswax (all right, a *lot* of beeswax), and putting fresh paper-hangings on the walls would go a long way towards making the old house shine like new again.

If only a jaded duke was so easy to fix, Hannah thought with a wistful twist of her mouth as she climbed a spiral staircase to the second floor. She walked slowly down the hall, her gaze drawn to the faded rectangles on the wall where she could only assume portraits used to hang. But of whom, and why had they been taken down? She doubted she'd get an answer from her husband. Maybe Peterson, although he struck her as the loyal sort who wouldn't divulge any information without his employer's consent. She had hoped to encounter a maid prone to gossip, but aside from the cook, a Frenchman who spoke very little English, Peterson was the only servant she had met.

Protocol dictated she receive a personal introduction to the household staff. Particularly since, as the duchess, she would be in charge of their daily tasks and schedules. But if Wycliffe had any intention of such an introduction, he had failed to mention it. A man of few words, her husband. And even fewer emotions. But like the house he had allowed to fall into neglect, he wasn't hopeless. There was more to him than the surly façade he presented to the world. Hannah was certain of it. His past experiences had made him hard and bitter, but even the hardest clay could be softened by the right hands.

The hall came to a dead end with one door on the left and another on the right. The door on the left opened to reveal a broom closet poorly stocked with supplies (unsurprising, given that the cleanliness of the house left much to be desired) and the door on the right refused to open at all. Wondering if it was locked or merely stuck, Hannah turned the knob and gave it a hard push. With a loud creak and a protesting groan the door swung inward to reveal a room so dark it was impossible to see more than a few inches in front of her face.

She would have thought it was another closet, except it was much too big. Stepping back out into the hallway, she retrieved a candle from one of the sconces on the wall and returned to the mysterious room. Mindful of the dripping wax, she held the candle high above her head, sending a spill of weak light across old wooden floorboards that were covered in dust and – she shuddered at the sight of them – rodent droppings.

There were no windows in the room and no furniture either save a single bed pushed up against the back wall. The mattress still had linens on it, although it was clear it had not been used in years, if not decades. It was also small, the size of a child's bed, although who would put a child in such a dark room so far away from all of the other bedchambers?

A floorboard creaked beneath the heel of her shoe as her curiosity drove her further into the room. She lifted her arm higher, sending light flickering up towards the ceiling. It was then she saw the most peculiar thing yet: two metal hooks that had been drilled into the middle of the ceiling. Spaced approximately two feet apart, each one had a small pulley with a rope attached to it.

"What in the world…" she breathed.

"They called it my rehabilitation room."

With a loud shriek Hannah spun around and nearly dropped the candle when she saw her husband looming in the doorway, his large frame casting a long rippling shadow across the floor. "You – you shouldn't sneak up on people like that!" she cried, flattening her palm against her chest where her heart was pounding against her ribcage. Wycliffe lifted a brow.

"And you shouldn't be sticking your nose where it doesn't belong. Who told you that you could come up here?"

"No one told me I *couldn't*." She took a deep breath. "What – what do mean, this was your rehabilitation room? I don't understand."

"I didn't either, at the time. Then again, I was just a young boy." He looked past her, the distant look in his eye revealing he wasn't seeing the room as it was now but as it had been. "My father was determined his one and only heir would not grow up to be a cripple, so he had this room constructed. I fell off a horse," he explained when his gaze shifted to Hannah and he saw her confusion. "One I never should have been riding, but I was an impulsive lad. The horse bolted across an open field and tripped in a hole. I would have been fine if I'd been thrown clear. A few bumps and bruises, perhaps a broken arm. But my foot caught in the stirrup iron."

Hannah muffled a gasp behind her hand. The corners of her husband's mouth lifted in a grim smile before he continued speaking in the flat, monotone voice of someone who was remarking on the weather instead of recalling a terrible childhood memory.

"I do not remember how long I was dragged. Honestly, I don't remember very much about the incident at all. Most of my recollection has come from what others have told me. When they found me I was unconscious. My right leg had been broken in three separate places and the horse's shoe had given me a nasty cut that eventually turned into this." He tapped the puckered scar on the side of his face. "For a while the doctor was convinced I was going to die. I was in so much pain I wished for death." He glanced up at the hooks. "But I didn't know what pain was. Not yet, at least."

“Is this where they kept you? After – after the accident?” Hannah couldn’t imagine condemning a child to such a bleak, windowless room. Particularly one who was so severely injured. Sunshine may have not been medicine for the body, but surely it was medicine for the soul.

“Not at first.” Wycliffe’s gaze lingered on the ceiling before it flicked to the bed. His jaw hardened. “But when my screams began to distract my father from his work, they moved me in here. It wasn’t just enough that I survived, you see. The duke did not want a cripple for his heir. He was determined I would return to the way I’d been before the fall. It did not occur to him, or perhaps he simply refused to acknowledge, that once bones have broken they can never be placed back exactly as they were. Although he did try.”

Wycliffe looked at Hannah then, and the bleakness she saw in the depths of his eyes made her heart ache. Without thinking she reached out and took his hand. For an instant his fingers entwined with hers and she felt the steady beat of his pulse before he abruptly yanked his arm away.

“Do not come in here again.” Any softness she might have glimpsed was gone, replaced with an icy indifference so cold she felt the chill of it beneath her clothes. He turned on his heel and limped away, leaving the door open behind him. After a few moments she followed and watched from the bannister as he walked stiffly down the stairs, her expression thoughtful.

For all his bristle and bluster, her husband had just revealed something that filled her with hope.

A crack in the ice around his heart.

CHAPTER SIX

WYCLIFFE COULD NOT remember the last time he'd spoken about his accident, and it infuriated him that he had revealed so much to Hannah. Particularly when he'd glanced up and seen the pity in those quiet gray eyes.

He did not want her *pity*. He did not want anything from her.

Except another kiss.

He stopped short, hands curling into fists as he closed his eyes and tried to banish any memory of their kiss from his mind.

It was a futile endeavor.

Try as he might (and he *had* tried) he could not forget the taste of her lips, or the satiny velvet of her skin, or the raspy mewling sound she'd made in the back of her throat when she came. Just thinking about it – the sight of her head thrown back in wild abandon, the sound of her desperate cries, the sweet scent of her desire – was enough to give him a bloody cockstand right there in the middle of the foyer. His raging arousal wasn't helped by the fact that he hadn't touched a woman in five years, and he'd *never* touched one he wanted as much as Hannah.

His gray-eyed, mousy little wife had gotten under his skin like no other woman since Lady Portia, and the knowledge both thrilled and terrified him.

Before Hannah showed up on his doorstep he'd been content in his life of solitude. Not happy – who needed happiness? – but content. Then she'd come barging in with her ridiculous proposal and instead of sending her away as he should have done, he'd invited her into the parlor. A fatal mistake, it seemed, for the instant she had revealed that if he did not marry her she would simply find someone else he'd been overcome with jealousy.

Marry someone *else*? He still bristled at the thought. Lord knew he hadn't been keen on the idea himself, but he'd be damned if he let another man have her. The foolish chit would have ended up getting herself hurt or worse going from door to door like some sort of common gypsy.

A chill racing down his spine as he imagined what might have happened if she'd knocked on the wrong one, Evan crossed the foyer and went into his study, closing the door firmly behind him.

He'd *saved* her. And how did she repay him? By

stirring up old memories and feelings long believed dead.

Sitting behind his desk, a twin pedestal mahogany piece that had once belonged to his father, he began to blindly flip through a stack of unopened letters, many of them dated months earlier. Peterson knew he never responded to mail, but the stubborn valet kept bringing it to him anyways in the hopes that the right correspondence might spark a renewed interest in returning to London. Evan snorted at the thought. He may have taken a bride, but if there was one thing he never had *any* intention of doing it was wading back into the swamp of high society.

"Tell the groom I will be there in a minute, Peterson," he said without looking up when he heard the door open. He'd planned a morning ride on his trusty old gelding (the only horse he knew with absolute certainty would never throw him, and one of only a few that tolerated his stiffness in the saddle), and had nearly been out the door when he'd heard the soft pitter-patter of footsteps in the east wing and had gone to investigate.

"Get off your lazy arse and tell him yourself." Sauntering into the study as if it were his own, the Duke of Colebrook winked one bright blue eye before collapsing onto an oversized leather chair and kicking his heels up on a corner table. "Darker than a witch's tit in here. Would it kill you to open a curtain and let in a little light?"

"You're welcome to leave if my choice of décor offends you," Evan growled. Colebrook's impromptu visits had long been a point of aggravation, but short of keeping the exterior doors locked at all times he had no way of preventing the duke from dropping in whenever he pleased.

"I came to offer my congratulations." Colebrook gave a winning smile. As fair as Evan was dark, his sandy blond hair was always expertly combed away from a face that could have made an angel swoon. Side by side, the two dukes could not have been more different. Colebrook was handsome, charismatic, and sociable. Evan was…none of those things. And yet for reasons that baffled Colebrook continued to stop by, seemingly determined to create a friendship that, if Evan had his way, would never exist.

"You've offered them." Shoving the stack of letters aside, Evan fixed his fellow duke with a frosty glare. "Now go away."

Still smarting from the last prank Colebrook had pulled – the one that had resulted in being awoken in the middle of the night by three drunken sailors belting out a lewd tune about a mermaid – he had no interest in playing the part of charitable host. Or any host, for that matter. As a man who valued his privacy, he did not take kindly to visitors. Particularly visitors who showed up whenever they pleased and refused to leave.

"Where is this lovely wife of yours I have heard so much about? You've got the entire village buzzing like a swarm of hornets." Colebrook's smile widened. "Won't be long before the *ton* catches word that the reclusive Duke of Wycliffe has finally tied the knot."

"And I'm sure you won't have anything to do with spreading the news," Evan said sourly.

"*Moi*?" Colebrook spread his fingers over his chest. "Wouldn't dream of it, old chap. Which is why I told my cousin not to breathe a word of it when he returned to London."

"I thought *you* were supposed to be London," Evan grumbled. Resigning himself to the fact that Colebrook had no intention of leaving anytime soon, he clasped his hands behind his head and leaned back in his chair. If he was going to be miserable for the undeterminable future then he might as well be comfortable.

"Had to return early." Colebrook's smile faded. "Some of the renovations with the estate went awry. Turns out one of the so-called architects I hired knew less about roof support than he let on. I won't bore you with the details–"

"Thank God for that."

"–but suffice it to say the entire bloody house is

unlivable until new beams can be put up. Which is why we're going to be roommates, old chap."

Evan leaned forward so quickly his teeth snapped together and he bit his tongue. Sucking furiously on the tiny cut, he stared at Colebrook in horrified disbelief. "The hell we are."

"I prefer a west-facing bedchamber. Sunsets are pretty enough, but sunrises?" The duke shook his head. "Those I prefer to sleep through. I've put up the majority of my staff in the village inn, but I'll need accommodations for my personal valet, footman, and cook. No offense intended, Wycliffe, but I've tasted that over-sauced rubbish your French chef dares to call food and I must say he's about as good at his job as my architect."

"You're not staying here and neither is your valet, your footman, or your bloody cook!" Evan rose out of his chair and leaned forward, knuckles gleaming white in the dim lighting as he braced his fingers on his desk. "This is not a damn hotel."

Colebrook frowned. "That's not very hospitable of you, Wycliffe. It is not as if you don't have the room. Why, this place is so big and empty you would hardly now I was even here."

"My answer is no," he said flatly. "Now kindly take your feet off my furniture and sod off."

"Sorry, old chap, but I can't do that." While

Colebrook's tone was vaguely apologetic, his blue eyes glittered with amusement. "Two carriages are on their way here as we speak. Just a few personal belongings, you understand. I can hardly be expected to live out of a single trunk now, can I?"

Evan grinded his teeth together with so much force he felt a distinctive pop in his jaw. Short of engaging Colebrook in fisticuffs (a fight he would almost certainly lose given his physical impairment) or shooting him outright (a compelling choice, although he feared he didn't have the temperament for prison) there was nothing he could do but allow Colebrook to stay.

But he didn't have to like it.

"I'll direct my butler to have your things delivered to the third floor when they arrive."

"Is there a west-facing bedchamber?"

For the first time since Colebrook had entered his study, Evan smiled. "There are several." There were also mice, cobwebs, and a leaky roof which was why the third floor had been sealed off for the better part of half a decade. "Take your pick. And please, if there is anything you need, do not hesitate to let my valet Peterson know."

Colebrook gave an approving nod. "Now that's more like it, Wycliffe. You know, I think this time together will be good for us. Strengthen our friendship and all that."

“Oh most definitely,” Evan said gravely. “If you’ll excuse me, I have a horse waiting.”

“Going for a ride?” Jumping to his feet with surprising quickness given his leisurely nature, Colebrook followed Evan to the door, the heels of his boots echoing on the wooden floor. “I’ll join you.”

“No. You won’t.” And without another word Evan walked through the door and shut it soundly in Colebrook’s face.

Chapter Seven

HANNAH SPENT THE rest of the day making lists. An organized person by nature, she had relied on lists from a very young age, first to catalog her doll collection and then to keep a running tally on all of her sister's extravagant purchases. Needless to say those lists had been quite long, but they were nothing compared to the one she was currently working on.

Remove and replace drapes in every room, it began in her neat, tidy handwriting.

Wash windows, repair cracked panes

New shutters – iron or wood?

Wash and polish floors

Beeswax!!

Dust ~~all sconces and chandeliers~~ everything

Replace candles

New furniture

New rugs

New paintings

And so the list went. On and on and on until it began to feel less like a list and more like a small novel.

Exhausted from climbing up and down countless flights of stairs (not to mention the sheer enormity of the tasks that laid ahead), she collapsed onto her bed and started to close her eyes, but no sooner had she drifted off to sleep than she was jolted awake by Elsbeth.

"You're not wearing *that* to dinner, are you? It's filthy." Charging into the room with all the discretion of a small but determined rhinoceros, the maid took one look at Hannah's dirt-streaked dress before she promptly went to the closet and pulled out a blue gown overlaid with sheer white muslin. "Quickly," she said when Hannah groaned and dragged a pillow over her head. "It wouldn't due to be late. You're a duchess now, you know."

Hannah *did* know, mostly because Elsbeth wouldn't let her forget. Being the personal maid of a gentlewoman was one thing, but being the maid of a duchess…well, that was something else entirely and Elsbeth was taking her elevated position *very* seriously. So seriously, in fact, that Hannah was tempted to offer Elsbeth the title if only to give herself a moment's peace and quiet.

"I believe I'll take supper in my room. I'm very tired."

Elsbeth clucked her tongue. "Don't be ridiculous. You

have a guest!"

"A guest?" The pillow tumbled to the floor as Hannah sat up and frowned. "What sort of guest?"

"A *duke*," her maid said importantly. Carefully draping the blue gown over the back of a chair so as not to wrinkle it, she motioned for Hannah to stand with an impatient flick of her wrist and whisked the soiled dress off her head. "The Duke of Colebrook, to be precise. He owns the neighboring estate."

Colebrook…Colebrook…the name sounded familiar, although she couldn't quite place it.

"Do you know what he's doing here?" she asked, recalling that her husband did not get many visitors. Which was not surprising, given the state of the manor. Who in their right mind would want to sleep amidst scurrying mice and sticky cobwebs? Three times she'd been woken by the sound of tiny claws scratching away in her closet which was why she now slept with a fire poker by her bed. Although hopefully as long as the mice kept to their end of the treaty she'd struck with them on her very first night – that was, to remain out of sight and out of anything that resembled a pocket – she'd never need to use it.

"Having dinner, I imagine." Climbing onto a three-legged stool, Elsbeth slid the new gown over Hannah's head whilst she stood with her arms straight up and her ankles touching, feeling for all the world like an awkward stork. "Then he must be spending the night because I saw one of the scullery maids bringing fresh linens up to the third floor."

"The third floor?" Hannah's nose wrinkled. "But it's filthy up there."

Tying off the gown at the neck and waistline, Elsbeth stepped down off the stool and lifted her shoulders in a small shrug. "Maybe they're cleaning it as well."

"Maybe," Hannah said doubtfully. To say the staff's work ethic was underwhelming was a grave understatement. From everything she'd witnessed, they were nothing short of lazy. And why wouldn't they be, when their employer didn't seem to care – or even notice – the two inches of dust coating every surface?

Her mother may have been a frivolous spender, but she'd always run a tight household. *'Tis the duty of every good wife*, she'd told her daughters on more than one occasion, *to give their husband sons and an orderly house.* Having failed to do the first, Lady Fairchild had seen to it their home was always impeccably turned out. Hannah could only hope to accomplish the same with Wycliffe Manor. A formidable task, but then she had always enjoyed a good challenge.

Standing patiently while Elsbeth pinned her hair back into a neat chignon that left two auburn tendrils dangling from either side of her temple, she finished her appearance with a pair of tiny pearl earrings – the only jewelry she'd brought with her – before heading to the dining room.

To her surprise, she arrived to find her husband already seated at the head of the long oak table where they'd been taking their supper – often separately. A blond man impeccably dressed in a white cravat and burgundy tailcoat sat to his right. They both rose when Hannah entered the room, but only the blond man (whom she assumed to be Colebrook) bowed.

"This must be your lovely duchess," he said, slapping a hand on Wycliffe's back. "Well done, old chap. She's a beauty."

Wycliffe's only response was a short grunt, but Hannah couldn't help but notice the way his gaze seemed to linger on her as she took her usual seat at the far end of the table. She offered him a tentative smile, to which he replied with a scowl. Resisting the urge to roll her eyes at his predictably curmudgeonly demeanor, she turned her attention to the first course of their meal, a piping hot bowl of boiled cauliflower and turmeric soup. But when it became apparent that Wycliffe and Colebrook intended to carry on a conversation without her – easy enough to do, given how far away she was – Hannah promptly picked up her soup and her spoon and sat down beside her husband.

"There," she said cheerfully, pretending not to notice Wycliffe's glowering stare. "Now we can converse without shouting. Tell me, Your Grace." She looked across the table at Colebrook. "How is it you know my husband?"

"We go way back," Colebrook said, a twinkle in his blue eyes. "Some might even call us childhood chums. Which was why I knew I could count on my old friend to put me up while my estate is undergoing renovations."

"Oh?" Pausing with the spoon halfway to her lips, Hannah glanced at her husband who was scowling into his bowl with such ferocity she wouldn't have been surprised if the soup curdled. "What sort of renovations?"

"All sorts." Colebrook waved his hand in the air. "I am afraid my grandfather was a bit of a gambler. Unfortunately, he wasn't very good at it and lost the family estate in a particularly unlucky hand of cards. I was able to reacquire the old girl some years ago, but haven't had the time to devote to her restoration until recently."

"How fortunate you were able to reclaim your childhood home," said Hannah.

"Indeed." There was a temporary lull in the conversation as their next course was served: roasted lamb covered in sweet cream sauce and asparagus sautéed in red onion with garlic. "So tell me," Colebrook said once the servants had left. "How is it you came to marry this grumpy old bastard?"

"Is he grumpy?" Hannah said innocently. "I hadn't noticed."

Tossing his head back, Colebrook laughed. "Beauty *and* wit. I quite like her, Wycliffe. You're a lucky man."

Suppressing a smile, Hannah stole a sideways glance at her husband. He sat stiffly in his chair, one hand wrapped around his fork while the other gripped his knife as if it were a deadly weapon. It was clear from his body language that he disliked Colebrook, but she couldn't imagine why. The other duke was friendly, warm, and amusing. In short, he possessed all of the qualities Wycliffe lacked. And yet as her gaze flicked back and forth between the two men, she found herself preferring her husband's dark, brooding nature over Colebrook's innate charisma.

Wycliffe may not have been outwardly charming. Or inwardly, for that matter. But there was something about him that pulled at her. She liked that he said what he thought. His opinion was not always been kind, but at least it was genuine. A babbling brook may have been pretty to look at but it was shallow and slight compared to a river which, while deeper and more treacherous, contained far more life within its watery depths.

"I am the lucky one," Hannah demurred.

Wycliffe's startled gaze rose from his plate to meet hers, a faint line appearing between his thick brows as they drew together over the bridge of his nose. His lips parted as if he were about to speak, but with a small, almost imperceptible shake of his head he took a bite of lamb instead.

Colebrook, having watched the subtle exchange with some interest, leaned back in his chair and changed the subject to the weather. For the rest of dinner he and Hannah maintained a polite discourse while Wycliffe ate in silence, his expression unreadable. Only when Colebrook offered to take Hannah down to the stables to show her his prized thoroughbred stallion did he finally speak.

"You'll not be taking my wife anywhere, Colebrook." His fist hit the table with more force than necessary, rattling the silverware and causing Hannah's brows to lift. If she didn't know any better she might be tempted to think there was a hint of jealousy in her husband's stormy blue eyes. But surely she was mistaken. For someone to be jealous of someone else they actually had to show interest in them, and ever since their kiss he had displayed a distinctive *lack* of interest. In fact, with the exception of their exchange earlier in the day, they'd hardly spoken more than a dozen words to one another since the day of their wedding!

"Perhaps you would like to take me," she said impulsively.

Wycliffe blinked. "Take you where?"

"To the stables, of course. I haven't seen them yet, and I would like to meet the horses. Unless you are too busy, in which case I am certain Colebrook would be delighted to accompany me." It was a dirty trick, to use one man against the other. One she'd seen deployed time and again but never tried to use herself…until now. *Desperate times*, she thought silently. If she didn't take the initiative with her marriage, who would? And if this was what it took to finally get her husband to notice her, well, then she wasn't above getting her hands a little dirty for once.

Colebrook stood up. "Wouldn't you know, there's something I've forgotten I need to do. Unless, that is, you need me to walk you down to the stables." He looked out the window. "It has gotten rather dark. I wouldn't want you to trip or lose your way."

"She doesn't need your help," Wycliffe growled. If he had hackles, they would have been standing on end. "If she wants go to the stables then I'll take her to the bloody stables."

It wasn't the most romantic invitation Hannah had ever received, but it was better than nothing. "Excellent!"

she said, jumping to her feet before he could change his mind. "Let's go."

"Now?" he said blankly.

For such an intelligent man, he was remarkably obtuse at times.

"It *is* getting rather dark. But if you're busy..."

"I will fetch your cloak," he said, jaw clenching as he shoved back from the table and stalked out of the room. Hannah bit her lip when the door slammed behind him and looked up uncertainly at Colebrook. Perhaps she'd made a mistake...but to her surprise, the other duke winked.

"Good job love," he said approvingly. "I've never seen the old chap in such a state before. You've not known each other for very long, have you?"

"We met on the same day we became engaged," Hannah confessed, her fingers twisting together in her lap. "It was a very...unusual circumstance."

"I can only imagine, seeing as Evan has sworn up and down he would never marry."

"Yes, he said as much. But I do not understand why." Hannah knew plenty of men who were reluctant to take the plunge into marital bliss – her sister's almost fiancé being one of them – but she'd never heard of a man who *never* wanted to get married. Especially a duke who did not yet have an heir.

"He didn't give you a reason?" Colebrook asked.

She shook her head. "Not specifically."

"Well, it is not my story to tell, but suffice it to say there was a woman." His mouth twisted in a humorless smile. "Isn't there always? And this woman received amusement at your husband's expense. It's funny."

"What is?" Hannah asked, for she found nothing the least bit humorous about what Colebrook had just told her.

"The things that stay with us." He was quiet for a moment, and she could tell that even though he was looking at her he wasn't really seeing her. Then he blinked, and his rakish smile returned just as the door swung back open.

"Are you coming or not?" Wycliffe demanded, holding up Hannah's cloak, an emerald green garment trimmed in soft gray fur. His gaze narrowed when he saw Colebrook was still in the room. "I thought you had a pressing matter to attend to."

"On my way," Colebrook said easily. As he walked behind Hannah's chair he leaned in close and whispered, "Good luck, love. You're going to need it."

Chapter Eight

Jealousy.

It wasn't an emotion Evan was accustomed to, and it wasn't one he liked. Yet all it had taken was the mere thought of Hannah alone in the stables with Colebrook for the green monster to raise its head, leaving him hard-pressed not to leap across the table and punch the smirk right off of Colebrook's bloody face.

He knew Hannah wouldn't betray him. His little wife was meek as a lamb and loyal besides. It was his lecherous, womanizing neighbor he didn't trust. He would rather cut off his good leg than leave Colebrook alone with his duchess for more than a few minutes, let alone allow him to drag her off into a dark, secluded barn. Which was why *he* was dragging her off into a dark, secluded barn.

Although God knew he wasn't happy about it.

There was a reason he'd been avoiding Hannah as if she carried the plague, and it wasn't because he did not like her. It was because he liked her *too* much.

One glance at her sunset colored hair, one whiff of her sweet floral scent, and he was hard as a rock and aching to take her into his arms. After being celibate for the better part of half a decade, it wasn't exactly a comfortable position to be in. Which was why he'd been doing his best to pretend she didn't exist. A difficult task to accomplish when he was in one wing of the house and she another; a damn near impossible one when they were walking side by side, her tiny hand buried in the crook of his elbow and her right breast temptingly close to brushing against his arm.

"I thought you'd been to see the horses before," he said as they walked slowly along a narrow, partially overgrown path that led from the manor down to the stables.

Originally made of wood, the main barn had burnt to the ground while Evan's grandfather was still alive and had been rebuilt out of stone. It was a two-story structure in the shape of an L with horses below and hay above. The longest part of the barn contained the stalls, each with a double hung door overlooking the front courtyard while the smaller section housed tack and feed. Behind the barn was a large paddock and beyond the paddock an even larger field.

During the warm summer months the horses were allowed out at night and kept in their stalls during the day to avoid the heat and the flies. But with the cooler temperatures they'd recently switched back to being stabled overnight and a chorus of sleepy whickers greeted Evan and Hannah when they reached the main entrance where twin lanterns cast a shallow circle of yellow light onto the freshly raked ground.

"No," she said, slipping her hand free of his arm in order to walk up to the nearest horse, an old bay mare named Abigail that had once belonged to Evan's mother. Laying a gloved hand alongside of Abby's neck, she gave the mare a gentle scratch. "I have never been a very accomplished rider, but I do enjoy their company. I believe it's their eyes."

"Their eyes?" Evan asked, his brow furrowing as he automatically reached into his pocket for a piece of peppermint and held it out to Abby who lipped up the treat with an appreciative snort and immediately began nosing his chest for more.

"A human can deceive you with their eyes, but not a horse." With one last pat Hannah moved on to the next stall. She giggled when its enthusiastic occupant, a dappled gelding with a mischievous nature, thrust his head over the door and knocked her bonnet askew. The happy sound, bright as a ray of sunshine on a clear summer's day, caught Evan off guard, as did the warmth that spread through his chest upon hearing it.

"That's true enough," he said tightly. Hannah peered at him from beneath the gelding's scruffy jaw, gray eyes big and bemused in the dim lighting.

"Is something the matter?" she asked.

Yes. Something bloody well is *the matter. I wasn't supposed to feel anything for you, and now I'm feeling too much. I wasn't supposed to want you, and now you're all I can think about. I wasn't supposed to believe in love, and now I think it might be the only thing worth believing in.*

"No," he snapped. "I am simply tired. I did not sleep well last night."

"Oh." Those soft, tempting pink lips pursed together and it was all he could do not to groan. "Would you like to return to the house?"

"You wanted to see the damn stables and we're seeing the damn stables. *Tonight*," he emphasized with so much force that Abby's ears flicked back and she bared her teeth. Hannah had a similar reaction.

"There's no need to be so short-tempered all of the time," she said, her tone gently chiding. "It was a simple question. Not an accusation."

He gritted his teeth. "I warned you that I was a bastard,

and a callous one besides. You knew exactly who I was when you married me."

"Yes," she acknowledged. "But you never told me *why* you are the way you are. Surely there must be a reason. Colebrook mentioned…"

"What?" he demanded when she hesitated. "Colebrook mentioned what? You cannot believe a word that lying bounder says. He'll try to turn you against me just for the amusement of it."

"Turn me against you?" This time when she looked at him, her eyes were sad. "I think you are doing a fine job of that all on your own, don't you?"

Evan's mouth opened. Closed. Her words had hit him like a punch to the gut, but before he could summon a response she'd moved on to the next stall.

"Who is this?" she asked, peering over the door at a spindly legged colt with a large white blaze and two white stockings. He was a handsome, inquisitive fellow, and – if he grew as tall as his sire – Evan's next riding horse. The colt's dam dozed in the corner, exhausted after a long day of chasing her impish offspring over hill and dale.

"He doesn't have a name yet." Evan joined her at the stall. She stepped sideways to accommodate him and her ankle turned. Without thinking he wrapped his arm around her waist to steady her. She fit against his side as if she'd been born to be there, her subtle curves as soft as feather down against the hard lines of his body. His jaw clenched. "Have I mentioned how much I dislike clumsy women?"

"Once or twice." Auburn curls spilled across his shoulder when she tilted her head back. In the soft glow of the lamplight the scattering of freckles across her nose and cheeks looked like tiny flecks of moon dust. "Have I mentioned how much I dislike rude, overbearing dukes?"

"Once or twice." *Let her go, damn you. Let her go now, while you still can.*

His grip tightened.

"Are you going to kiss me again?" she whispered, her eyes two shimmering pools of ash beneath a thick fringe of velvet lashes.

"Do you want me to?" His voice was hoarse, his blood hot.

"Yes." Her tongue slipped between her lips, drawing his gaze down to her delectable little mouth. A mouth that was all but begging to be tasted. By *him*. And if that wasn't the most confounding thing on God's green earth he didn't know what was.

Hannah wanted him. The half crippled duke with a disfigured face who'd once been mocked by the entire *ton*. He didn't know why or how, given as he did not even want himself. But she did.

And he wanted her.

He wanted her more than he'd ever wanted anything in his entire life. More than he'd wanted to walk. More than he'd wanted his father's approval. More than he'd wanted the echoes of Lady Portia's cruel laughter to disappear. And so with a savage growl that was more beast than man, he took what he wanted.

Chapter Nine

IF THEIR LAST kiss had set Hannah's body on fire, then this one threatened to burn her to the ground. On a delighted gasp she parted her lips, allowing her husband's tongue to sweep boldly into her mouth as she shoved her fingers into his hair.

Easily spanning her waist with both hands, Wycliffe turned her in his arms so they were face to face, chest to chest, groin to groin. She felt the throbbing pulse of his arousal through his trousers. Felt an answering dampness between her thighs that brought a warm blush to her cheeks.

After their passionate exchange in the goldenrod she thought she'd known what to expect the next time he kissed her.

But she was wrong.

So utterly, completely, delightfully wrong.

His hands slid up to cup her breasts, thumbs brushing across her nipples as he tilted his head and deepened the kiss. She let go of his hair to clutch at his nape, fingernails digging furrows in his skin through the silk fabric of her gloves.

He bit down on her bottom lip and she whimpered.

He licked the tiny bite and she moaned.

Sensation after sensation washed over her until she was drowning in desire. Her entire body hummed with it, and when he backed her against the rough barn wall and shoved up her skirts to stroke the wettest part of her she clenched around his finger almost immediately, stars bursting behind her closed eyelids as he ruthlessly drove her to the pinnacle of wild abandon and shoved her over the edge.

He softened her fall with a kiss, murmuring quiet, unintelligible words of comfort against her swollen lips as she clung to his neck as if it were a sturdy mast in a deep, turbulent sea. When the waters began to calm she opened her eyes to find him staring down at her, his own gaze as dark as the sea she'd just lost – and found – herself in.

"Again," he said simply, and before Hannah could fully comprehend what he meant he had slipped his finger back inside of her and captured her mouth in a long, drugging kiss that did not end until she was crying out his name.

"*Wycliffe. Wycliffe.*" It spilled from her lips like a chant as he brought her to the top of the mountain again and again, until her knees were weak and her body was trembling and she could barely remember her own name.

Then *she* was touching *him*, her fingers taking on a life of their own as she freed him from the front flap of his trousers. He spilled hot and heavy into her hands, the tip of his phallus damp with desire.

"I don't know what to do," she whispered. In response he wrapped his hand around hers and guided her palm along his hard length until he'd established a rhythm that quickened with every stroke.

"Like that," he rasped, and Hannah experienced a thrill of delight when she realized she was bringing him the same erotic pleasure he had brought her.

His head fell back, Adam's apple bobbing as the muscles in his abdomen went rigid. When he found his release he groaned her name – the very first time he'd ever spoken it – and her heart filled with a cozy warmth that had nothing to do with lust and everything to do with love.

Their heavy breaths intermingled with the quiet snorts and whickers of the horses as they both slowly descended back to earth. Removing a monogrammed handkerchief from the front pocket of his waistcoat Wycliffe offered it to her first but with a shy shake of her head she declined, unable to meet his gaze for fear of what she would see in the cool depths of his eyes.

Would he reject her, as he had before? Or would this time be different? Would this time he finally admit when she knew – or at least, she hoped – he felt in his heart? For surely he could not have kissed her like he had, touched her like he had, brought her pleasure like he had…if he didn't feel *something* for her.

She had her answer after he was done cleaning himself up. Stuffing the handkerchief back into his pocket and buttoning his trousers he stepped back, and her heart sank all the way down to her toes when she saw the rigid line between his brows.

"I am sorry," he said stiffly. "That should not have–"

"Devil take your apology!" She threw her hands in the air, spooking the nameless colt. He spun in a circle in his stall, but Hannah was too incensed to notice. "And devil take you! I – you – *oh*!" Unable to put her anger into words, she shoved past him and ran all the way back to the manor, her tears glistening like diamonds in the moonlight.

HANNAH DID NOT speak a word to Wycliffe for the next three days. She couldn't. She was too furious with him.

Furious that he'd brought her so much pleasure…and

furious that he'd brought her so much pain. How could he have filled her with fire one moment and treated her with such infuriating coldness the next? And his blasted apology! Her jaw still clenched whenever she thought of it. She didn't want his apology. She wanted *him.* And more than ever before she wanted to know what had happened in his past to have left him with such horrific scars.

Not the ones on his face. Those had healed years ago and as much as he seemed to believe otherwise, they did not bother her in the slightest. No. It was the scars he carried on his frozen heart that concerned her. Scars that were still bleeding even after all this time.

Her marriage to Wycliffe may have saved her family from financial ruin and her father from debtor's prison, but at what cost to herself? Was she destined to be forever trapped in a loveless union? One made all the worse because she feared she *was* falling in love with her husband…and, even though he would never admit it, he was falling in love with her as well.

He hadn't said the words – hadn't even come close – but she knew, she *knew* that he couldn't kiss her such wicked abandon if he didn't care deeply for her.

Some men could have. Men like Colebrook, who saw every woman they met as a conquest to be won. But not Wycliffe. If what he felt towards her was nothing more than lust then he would have no reason to apologize. After all, she was his wife. His property before God and country. If he wanted her in his bed he did not have to ask, and he certainly did not have to apologize. That he had done so – twice – gave her hope there was more to his feelings than what he showed on the surface.

But her hope was rapidly dwindling, and her mood was certainly not improved by her sister's unexpected arrival.

"He's called off the engagement!" Cadence wailed, her tearful voice echoing in the vast emptiness of the manor as she ran across the foyer and straight into Hannah's arms. The footman who had admitted Cadence regarded the sister's reunion with wide eyes before he promptly slipped out the door and shut it firmly behind him, leaving them alone.

"Who has?" Hannah said, caught off guard not only by Cadence's sudden appearance but also her state of dishevelment. With her silky brown hair is wild disarray and her eyes red and swollen from crying, Cadence looked nothing like the calm, composed bride-to-be Hannah had left in London.

"Who?" her sister repeated shrilly. "Who do you think? Lord Benfield! Lord Benfield has called off our engagement!"

"Perhaps it would be best if you sat down. Come, over

here." Gently guiding Cadence into the parlor and over to a settee that was only moderately dusty, she sat down beside her and turned so they were facing one another. "Now take a deep breath," she said firmly. "And tell me what happened. I thought you and Lord Benfield were not yet engaged? How could he call off your engagement?"

"We were *practically* engaged!" Cadence cried. "Everyone knew it was only a matter of time."

Everyone, apparently, except for Lord Benfield, Hannah thought silently. Truth be told she'd never liked the earl, but Cadence had seemed quite smitten with him and so she'd bitten her tongue. Now, however, she saw no reason to continue hiding her dislike.

"Good." She patted her sister's knee. "You are far better off without him."

"Better off?" Cadence's dark gray eyes widened in disbelief. "Better off? I'm ruined, Han! Completely ruined."

"Oh, I wouldn't say–"

"He might as well left me at the a-altar. I will never love again." And with that rather bold proclamation, Cadence abruptly buried her face in her hands and burst into tears.

"What the devil is going on in here?" Appearing in the doorway, Wycliffe took one look at Cadence and immediately stepped back into the hall. Her mouth settling in a mulish frown, Hannah sprang to her feet and followed him out, closing the door behind her so Cadence could not overhear their conversation.

"That is my sister. She's going to be staying with us." She lifted a challenging brow, daring her husband to contradict her. She was tired of being understanding and finished with being patient. If Wycliffe was going to a stubborn arse despite her best attempts to coax a bit of humanity out of him, then she was done trying.

Hadn't she learned her lesson with her sisters and her dear father? No matter how many times she told them to stop wasting money, no matter how many different ways she pleaded with him to enforce stricter allowances, they never listened and they certainly never changed. Why had she expected Wycliffe to be any different? For better or worse, people were who they were. Unfortunately for her, she'd married someone who fell decidedly into the 'worse' category.

Which was why she was so utterly shocked when he looked at the parlor where Cadence's loud sobs could be heard clearly through the door and then back at Hannah before he inclined his head and said, quite simply, "All right."

Then he turned and walked away towards his study, leaving Hannah gaping after him.

"Wait!" she called, but he didn't so much as pause.

Running back into the parlor, she pressed a quick kiss to Cadence's damp cheek and promised she'd return promptly before dashing after her husband.

She reached him just as he was about to close the door to his study, and quickly slipped into the dimly lit room before he could slam the door in her face. It took a moment for her eyes to adjust to the darkness and when they did she discovered Wycliffe frowning at her from behind his desk, arms folded across his chest and a formidable line entrenched between his dark brows.

"Is there something I can help you with?" he growled.

"Why is every room in this house so very d-dark?" Just a little breathless from her impromptu sprint through the manor, Hannah turned in a slow circle, frowning when she saw the heavy drapes covering the windows.

She'd managed to replace the drapes in her bedchamber and drawing room with blue silk curtains Elsbeth had found in the attic and was waiting for a shipment to arrive from London before she moved on to the other rooms in the manor. She had also hired three new maids and was actively looking for a new housekeeper. Preferably one who did not take naps in the broom closet with a bottle of rum.

Slowly but surely the old house was emerging from the shadows, but she'd not yet dared to change so much as a piece of parchment in her husband's study.

"It's the middle of the day, yet being in here you would never know it." Crossing to the nearest window she drew back the drape and squinted up at the bright autumn sun. Over the past few days the air had grown noticeably colder. There were now more leaves on the ground than there were on the trees, and the berries on the holly bushes had started to turn orange. By the end of the month they would be bright red and then it was only a matter of time before the winds began to howl and snow started to fall.

"Don't you miss the light?" she asked, letting the drape fall back into place to glance at Wycliffe over her shoulder.

"I grew accustomed to the dark a long time ago," he said, bracing his hands on the edge of the desk.

Hannah thought of the room she'd discovered in the forbidden east wing. The one without windows and the strange metal hooks in the ceiling. A shiver went down her spine. "How long did they keep you in there?"

She could tell by the narrowing of his eyes that he knew exactly what she was talking about, and he wasn't pleased with the question.

"Long enough," he said shortly.

"How long?" she pressed.

"Two years."

"Two *years*!" Her horrified gaze flew to his as she

whirled around. "You were only a child. That must have been–"

"Barbaric? Cruel? Inhumane?" His mouth twisted in a humorless smile. "It was all that and more. But in the end I walked again. I wasn't a cripple. Or at least not a complete cripple. And that was all my father cared about."

"He sounds like he was a horrible man," Hannah whispered, unable to imagine her own father condemning her to such a fate. Lord Fairchild may have been absentminded and incapable of managing a budget, but he loved his family with all of his heart and he would never purposefully bring any harm to them. No wonder Wycliffe was capable of such callousness. He'd learned it at his sire's knee.

"My father was a duke," Wycliffe said, as if that explained everything.

"So are you," Hannah pointed out. And as cold and abrasive as he'd been towards her, she refused to believe he would ever lock an innocent child away in a windowless room and force them to endure all manner of horrific treatments.

"Not by choice, or by practice. Why do you think I live all the way out here?"

"Because you don't like anyone?" she guessed.

"I like you." The unexpected admission caught them

both by surprise. His face turning a dull ruddy color, Wycliffe made an awkward show of straightening a pile of letters. "What do you want?" he said without looking at her. "Why have you come in here?"

"My sister." As if pulled by an invisible thread, Hannah slowly started to walk towards him, her soft-soled shoes sinking silently into the worn carpet. "Why would you allow her to stay here? I know how much you dislike visitors."

"She is your sister," he muttered. "I know how important family is to you."

Three more steps and she would be at the desk.

One...

"How do you know that?" she asked.

Two...

He folded a letter into a tiny square. Unfolded it. Folded it again. "Because you were willing to marry a complete stranger to save them. There are not many daughters who would think to do that. Even fewer who would actually follow through with it."

Three...

"Look at me, Evan." She spoke so softly that she didn't think he heard her until, with obvious reluctance, he lifted his chin. A lock of hair tumbled into his eyes. With an irritated shake of his head, he tossed it back.

"What?" he said roughly. "What the bloody hell do

you *want*?"

Reaching across the desk, she placed her hand on top of his, fingers fitting perfectly between the grooves of his knuckles. "I want a husband who loves me. I want a marriage that means something. I want a partner, not a business arrangement."

Midnight blue eyes searching hers, he swallowed hard. "Hannah, I–"

"Why is there a sobbing woman in the parlor?" Barging into the study without bothering to knock, Colebrook stopped short at the sight of Hannah and Wycliffe leaning towards one another over the desk. "Oh. Bloody hell. I didn't…that is to say, I should have…"

"Knocked?" Wycliffe said icily, his gaze still on Hannah. "Get out, Colebrook."

"Of course. Right away." The blond duke started to back out the door. "Er, if someone could tell me who that woman is–"

"Get *out*," Wycliffe snarled.

"Aye," Colebrook said hastily. "I'll just, ah…go about my business and you two…er…carry on doing whatever it was you were, ah, doing. Cheerio."

"You were saying?" Hannah said quietly once they were once again alone.

"Nothing." Sliding his hand out from beneath hers, Wycliffe took a step back as an all too familiar shadow flickered over his face. “It was nothing.”

“Wait.” Desperate not to lose the softness she’d glimpsed on his face before Colebrook – damn him! – had interrupted them, Hannah hurried around the edge of the desk and grabbed onto his arm, fingers squeezing tight. “Please look at me. I know you feel something for me. I felt it the first time we kissed and again in the stables. Maybe it’s not love, but it could be. It *could* be, and I–”

“Please release my arm, Miss Fairchild.”

“Wait! If you would just listen to me and what’s in your heart, then I know–”

“You’re the one who has not listened,” he said icily. “I told you what this marriage would be before we ever walked down the aisle, and you agreed to it. I thought you were a woman of your word.”

“I am. I *am*, but if you would just–”

“Release my arm,” he repeated between gritted teeth, “and kindly remove yourself from my study. I have work to do.”

Hannah wanted her husband, but she would not beg for him. Gray eyes bright with tears she refused to let fall, she left the study – and any remaining hope she might have had that Wycliffe was capable of changing – behind.

Chapter Ten

"I SAY, DO you need a handkerchief? Although at the rate you're going, might I suggest a towel. Mayhap two."

Choking back a sob, Cadence looked up through bleary eyes to see a tall, broad-shouldered man standing in the doorway. His blond hair was swept back from his face to reveal a distinguished forehead, thick brows several shades darker than his hair, clear blue eyes, a straight nose, and a full, sensual mouth that was curved in a faintly mocking grin.

He was stunningly handsome and (if his smirk was any indication) he knew it. Was *this* the reclusive Duke of Wycliffe? The one whose hideousness was rumored to have cracked every mirror in his manor? Surely not. And yet, who else could it be?

Hastily wiping away her tears, Cadence pushed off the settee and bent her knees in a small, stiff curtsy. The journey here had been far longer and more arduous than she'd expected. In hindsight she probably would have done a great deal better to visit her aunt in Huffs Church, but when Benfield ripped her heart out of her chest and proceeded to stomp it into a thousand tiny little pieces the only person she'd wanted to see was Hannah.

"I apologize for my intrusion, Your Grace. Due to some…unforeseen circumstances" – that was one way to put it, being left humiliated and brokenhearted was another – "I needed to leave London."

The duke's gaze dropped to her belly. "In the family way, are you?" he said sympathetically. "I knew it the moment I saw you. Don't worry, love. There are plenty of nice villagers who would be happy to raise a squalling brat. I can provide a list if you'd like."

"What? No!" Flattening her hands over her stomach, she stared at Hannah's husband in disbelief. "I'm not – that is to say, I am not *pregnant*," she hissed, a blush overwhelming her cheeks. "And even if I were, I would not let my child be raised by *strangers*."

Good heavens. Who had she told her sister to marry?

"No need to be sod dramatic, love. It is not as if they would *eat* the child." The duke rolled his eyes. "It's a perfectly practical solution to an unfortunate problem. But if you are not expecting–"

"I am not," Cadence said firmly.

"–then you have nothing to worry about."

Except, apparently, the fact that she *looked* pregnant. Which, in the grand scheme of things, was somewhere below Never Being Able to Show Her Face in London Again and above Losing Her Second Favorite Pair of Gloves.

"Do you know where my sister is?" she asked.

The duke blinked. "Why the devil would I know where your sister is?"

Cadence frowned. "Why *wouldn't* you know?"

"Because I don't know *who* your sister is? Or who you are, for that matter." He stepped further into the parlor, a rakish gleam entering his eyes. "Except for one of the most beautiful women I've ever seen." Gaze intent on her mouth, he reached for a loose tendril of hair dangling down over her shoulder. Cadence slapped his hand away in shock.

"Your Grace!" she gasped. "You are married to my sister."

"The devil I am." Rearing back on his heels, the duke regarded her with a scowl. "Are you deaf or otherwise mentally impaired? I told you not two seconds ago that I didn't know who the bloody hell your sister was."

The poor man. Cadence knew the duke's accident had left his body scarred, but she'd had no idea it had addled his mind.

"You should get some rest," she said kindly. "When my uncle becomes confused he often takes a nap and feels much better afterwards. He also drinks a special tea, although I cannot recall the ingredients at the moment."

The duke's blue eyes flashed. "I am not confused. And I do not need a bloody nap or any of your damned witchcraft tea, for that matter."

Cadence's cheeks flushed. "It's not witchcraft tea. And you should not use such vulgar language in the presence of a lady!"

"When I see one I'll be sure to keep that in mind," he sneered.

"Oh!" she gasped. "You are the most wretched, appalling, *arrogant–*"

"Finally, a woman who sees you for who you truly are." A second man strolled into the parlor and all it took was one glance at the gruesome scar running down one side of his face for Cadence to realize her mistake.

"You're not the Duke of Wycliffe," she said accusingly, glaring at the blond-haired stranger who she'd confused for her sister's husband.

"Bloody hell, I should hope not." he said with a shudder.

"Miss Fairchild, might I introduce you to my temporary houseguest, the Duke of Colebrook. He is staying here while his estate undergoes renovations."

"I would say it is a pleasure to make your acquaintance, Your Grace," Cadence said icily. "But my mother always told me it was impolite to tell a lie."

"Allow me to show you to your rooms, Miss Fairchild." Mouth twitching with thinly concealed amusement, Wycliffe extended his arm. Sailing past Colebrook with her nose in the air, Cadence allowed her brother-in-law to escort her out of the parlor and up the stairs.

Unable to shake the feeling of eyes upon her, however, she paused at the top of the staircase and glanced back over her shoulder. There, in the middle of the foyer, stood Colebrook. When he saw her looking down at him he bent forward in a mocking bow and, without taking his burning gaze off of her, straightened and blew her a kiss.

"Just ignore him," Wycliffe provided helpfully. "I do."

Taking the duke's advice, Cadence turned and followed him down the hall. But she couldn't help but wonder what Colebrook's kiss had meant…and when she would see him again.

TO SAY THAT evening's dinner was a frosty affair would have been a grave understatement.

Hannah glared at Wycliffe.

Wycliffe glared at Colebrook.

Colebrook glared at Cadence.

And Cadence, having finally sorted out who was who, glared right back at Colebrook.

Conversation, when it occurred, was kept to such benign topics as the weather and the pending autumn harvest. And no sooner had dessert been finished than everyone retreated to their separate bed chambers.

To Hannah's surprise, she slept rather well. Tucked beneath layers of blankets and warmed by a fire smoldering in the hearth, she did not wake until dawn. For a moment she considered trying to fall back asleep, but then with a shrug and a stretch she tossed back the covers and tip-toed across the icy floor to her wardrobe. If there was one benefit of being up with the sparrows, it was that everyone else – including her husband – was almost certain to still be in their beds. A good thing, as the only company she currently sought was that of herself and the horses.

Last night before bed she'd asked a scullery maid to set aside some of the carrots from the soup. When she opened her door she found them waiting for her as requested inside a small burlap sack. Tucking the sack under her arm she proceeded downstairs, careful to walk on her tiptoes so as not to rouse Cadence who was sleeping just across the hall.

Her husband's valet, a perpetual early riser, greeted her in the foyer with a respectful bow. She'd not had the opportunity to exchange more than a few words with Peterson since coming to Wycliffe Manor, but she liked him for his loyalty and kind demeanor.

"Good morning, Your Grace. Going out for an early walk?" Peterson asked, taking note of the hooded cloak she'd thrown on directly over her nightdress. Scuffed leather boots peeked out from the satin hem and her hair was concealed beneath a wide-brimmed bonnet lined with soft ermine.

"Just to the stables. I've treats for the horses." She lifted the carrot filled sack. "Do you know if they've been turned out for the day?"

"Not to my knowledge. Would you like me to see if His Grace is able to accompany you?"

"No," Hannah said quickly. *Too* quickly she realized when a flicker of concern passed over Peterson's usually stalwart countenance.

"Might I have permission to make a very personal observation, Your Grace?"

Hannah eyed Peterson warily. "I suppose."

"I have known the duke for a very long time. You could almost say we grew up together, as my father served his until the day he died. And during all those years, I have never seen His Grace look at a woman the way he looks at you."

"Oh." A warm blush stole across Hannah's cheeks.

Biting her lip, she looked down at the floor. "Mr. Peterson, I am sorry to say but I think you are mistaken. My husband is not – that is to say, we're not…he doesn't love me," she blurted out, and to her horror she felt the sharp sting of tears in the corners of her eyelids.

"Your Grace?" Visibly alarmed by her sudden display of emotion, Peterson took a step back. "Should I send for your lady's maid?"

"No. No, I – I want to speak to you." Sniffling, Hannah lifted her sleeve and blew loudly into it. "You said it yourself, you've known Wycliffe for a very long time. Perhaps longer than anyone else. Can you tell me why he is the way he is? Please," she begged when the valet started to shake his head. "I want to understand. I *need* to understand. You're the only one who can help me."

Peterson was quiet for a long moment. So quiet that Hannah feared he was going to deny her request. But with a quiet sigh and a quick glance around to ensure they were alone, he leaned in close. "I don't know all the details. I was not there when it happened, but I saw him directly after and the humiliation and devastation on his face is something I will never forget." He took a deep breath before he continued grimly, "There was a young lady, at a ball. One that His Grace regarded quite favorably. He believed she regarded him the same way, but after they danced he discovered it had been nothing more than a bet."

"A bet?" Hannah asked, auburn brows drawing together in confusion.

"Apparently the young lady, along with her friends, had placed a bet amongst themselves. The one who danced with His Grace the longest was the winner."

"I – I still don't understand."

"No," said Peterson. "I wouldn't expect you to. These *ladies,* and I use the term loosely, saw the duke as nothing more than a freak. They made the bet to amuse themselves, not because they had any real interest in him. And in doing so they managed to reinforce all of the horrific things his father had said to him over the years. Things I will not repeat in polite company. Suffice it to say His Grace was left with the impression that no woman would ever be able to see past his scars, or love him for who he was on the inside." The valet straightened. "Does that answer your question, Your Grace?"

"Yes, I think it does." *Cruelty on top of cruelty*, Hannah thought silently, her chest aching for the young boy who had suffered so much pain and the young man who had been mocked for it. No wonder her husband did not trust anyone. Those he loved had disappointed and hurt him at every turn when they should have been protecting him. "Thank you, Mr. Peterson."

"Do not give up on him, Your Grace," the valet said earnestly. "He is a good man with a good heart."

Hannah smiled sadly. "I know. What I *don't* know is if my heart is strong enough to fix his."

Chapter Eleven

"PETERSON, HAVE YOU seen my wife?" Evan had been looking for Hannah for nearly an hour. After a restless night spent tossing and turning and going over their last conversation again and again, he had finally reached a few conclusions. The principle among them being that he'd treated his wife poorly, and he needed to apologize. But after looking everywhere he could think of including her bedchamber, the library, even the dreaded east wing – he was no closer to finding her than when he'd started.

There was one thing he *had* discovered on his search, however.

Light.

It streamed into the manor from all directions, illuminating the freshly swept floors and polished wood trim and the new furniture in nearly every room. Or mayhap it was simply old furniture that had been uncovered and cleaned; either way, he felt as if he was walking through someone else's house. Hannah's house, to be more precise.

While he had been stomping about, grumpy as a bear and glowering at anyone and everyone who crossed his path, she had been pouring her heart and soul into Wycliffe Manor. His little wife had managed to turn the old, dusty heap of bad memories into something any duke would be proud to call home.

He wanted to tell her how pleased he was with all of her hard work. He wanted to tell her he was sorry for the way he had acted in the stables and his study. Most importantly, he wanted to tell her that she was right and he was wrong. About so many things.

But to do all that, he had to find her first.

"Well?" he asked, hands settling low on his hips. "Have you seen the duchess or not?"

"She's gone, Your Grace." Peterson frowned. "I'm sorry, I assumed you knew."

Evan didn't like the finality in his valet's tone. And he sure as hell didn't like his use of the word 'gone'.

"Gone?" he growled. "What the devil do you mean, she's gone? Gone where?"

"I – I couldn't say, Your Grace. She left early this morning. At daybreak."

"And you didn't think to *tell* me?"

Peterson met his employer's furious gaze without blinking. "To be honest, Your Grace, I did not think you would care."

"Well you thought wrong," Evan snarled.

"Might I ask where you are going?" Peterson called after him as he threw open the door and stormed out into the brisk autumn air.

"To get my damn wife back."

"YOU'RE HERE."

Turning at the sound of her husband's stupefied voice, Hannah tucked a loose piece of hair behind her ear and frowned. "Of course. Where else would I be?"

"I thought…Never mind." With a hard shake of his head, Wycliffe walked around a bale of straw and into the stables, the shoulders of his coat slightly damp from the misting rain that had just started to fall. Inside the barn it was warm and cozy and the smell of leather lingered pleasingly in the air.

"What are you doing?" he asked.

"Feeding the horses." Picking up the nearly empty sack, she held it out. "There's still a few carrots left if you'd like to join me."

Standing shoulder to shoulder, they walked slowly down the long row of stalls, neither one of them speaking. When the last carrot had been given out to a pretty sorrel with one brown eye and one blue, Hannah finally gathered the courage to face her husband.

She'd been thinking hard about what Peterson had told her. The glimpse into Wycliffe's past had given her a piece of the puzzle she'd desperately needed, but it hadn't solved it for her. For that she needed her husband. But did he need her?

"When I came here, I did so out of sheer desperation," she began quietly. "I didn't know anything about you except what I had heard through rumors and conjecture. Still, I thought I knew what to expect." Biting her lip, she looked up to find him gazing down at her, his steely gaze unreadable. "But I was wrong."

Wycliffe's jaw clenched. "Because I was even more hideous than you were led to believe?"

"Because you were even more handsome," she corrected. When he made a scoffing sound of disbelief under his breath she removed her glove and slowly, gently, traced his jagged scar with the tips of her fingers. "Beauty is not defined by our outward appearance. Those who think otherwise are cruel and smallminded."

"I am a cripple," he said shortly.

"Is that what you see when you look at yourself in the mirror? Because I see a man who is capable of more than he knows. You're just wrapped in so much armor and ice that you can't see it for yourself." She knew she'd struck a nerve when she saw the flash of pain his eyes.

"You're afraid," she whispered, her thumb resting against the raised edge of his scar as she cradled his cheek in her palm. "Afraid I will hurt you like your father did for putting you through such horrific treatments, and your mother for not stopping him, and the women for mocking you."

Wycliffe's gaze darkened. "Colebrook told you about Lady Portia?"

"No, Mr. Peterson did. But *you* should have. You're my husband, Evan, and I am your wife. If we cannot share our secrets and our pain and our deepest desires with one another, then who can we share them with?"

"I don't know," he said bleakly. "I've never...I've never had anyone I can trust."

Trust me. Love me. Choose me over them. Choose our future over your past.

"I cannot promise I will never hurt you," she said quietly. "I'm sure I do not need to tell you this, but you are a *very* infuriating man. And I know that we will argue and say things we don't mean. But I swear that no matter what happens, no matter how angry you make me or how hard you try to push me away, I will never leave you in the dark."

"Hannah." It was only the second time he'd ever spoken her name, and it was even more meaningful than the first. “Hannah, I don’t deserve you. The way I’ve acted…the things I’ve said…”

“Were hurtful. I won’t deny it. But at least now I can understand why you said them.”

He placed his hand over top of hers, pressing her fingers into his scar. “Can you forgive me?”

“Yes, I can. I have.” She took a deep breath, preparing herself for rejection even as she hoped and prayed for acceptance. “I love you Evan.”

“I love you Hannah,” he said simply, and her heart swelled with so much happiness it was a wonder she could contain it all. “I think I have loved you from the first moment you showed up on my doorstep, but I was too bloody stubborn and scared to admit it. Everyone I have ever loved has brought me nothing but heartache and pain. But you, Hannah…” Lowering his head, he claimed her lips in a kiss so soft and gentle it brought tears to her eyes. “You’ve given me nothing but light.”

When they walked out of the stables the rain had ceased and the sun was beginning to emerge. Stopping suddenly, Hannah pointed up at the sky above Wycliffe Manor.

“Look!” she exclaimed. “A rainbow. Isn’t it beautiful?”

“Not as beautiful as my duchess,” Evan said huskily. And taking her in his arms, he kissed her again.

Epilogue

One Week Later

"Are you certain you will be all right here by yourself?" Hannah fretted. "There is plenty of room in the carriage. You could always accompany us, you know."

"On your honeymoon?" Cadence shook her head. "I think not. I will be perfectly fine remaining here. Elsbeth will be with me and besides, you'll only be gone for a fortnight. It will give me time to catch up on my reading."

Hannah regarded her sister dubiously. "You hate reading."

"My sleeping, then. And we both know how much I like that. Go." Looking out the window at the gleaming black coach where the Duke of Wycliffe was impatiently waiting for his bride to join him, Cadence gave Hannah a gentle push. "Enjoy your time alone together."

"Very well." Hannah did not need any more urging than that. Pressing a chaste kiss to Cadence's cheek, she whirled around and all but ran out the door. Her husband met her halfway and she squealed in delight when he picked her up in his arms and whirled her around before helping her up into the carriage.

Cadence watched wistfully as they rolled down the long drive and out of sight. She was happy for her sister, but she couldn't help but feel a touch envious as well. A perfectly understandable emotion, she supposed, given the circumstances.

Lingering at the window for a few more minutes, she finally turned and headed for the stairs. Truth be told she didn't know *how* she was going to occupy her time over the next two weeks; all she knew was that it was better to be here than in London. Wycliffe Manor may have been in the middle of nowhere, but that was what made it so appealing: she was far, far away from the mocking whispers of her peers.

"Going back to your room to mope about and eat more chocolate?" a masculine voice drawled as she passed by the parlor. Cadence stopped and looked in through the open doorway. There, draped lengthwise across a chaise lounge and looking every inch the wicked, rakish scoundrel that he was, laid the Duke of Colebrook.

Drats. She's completely forgotten he would be staying here as well; the renovations on his estate having not yet been completed. For a moment she considered chasing after the newlywed's carriage before she dismissed the idea as folly. For one thing, she'd never catch it. For another, the estate was large enough for two people to avoid each other if they wanted to. And she dearly, dearly wanted to.

There was just something about Colebrook that got under her skin, like a splinter she couldn't quite reach. Every time she tried to yank the splinter out it embedded itself even further and she was left grinding her teeth in frustration, wondering if she'd ever be able to remove it.

"I have nothing to say to you," she said crossly.

Chuckling under his breath, Colebrook sat up. "Poor Miss Fairchild. Ever the brokenhearted damsel in distress. Do you know the best way to get over someone you used to love?" he asked.

Ignore him, Cadence ordered herself. *Ignore him and keep walking.*

"What is that?" she said with a jaunty toss of her head.

"Kiss someone you don't." His smirking grin fading as he stared at her with eyes that were dark with lust and some other emotion she couldn't quite decipher, he slowly uncoiled his lanky frame and stood up. "Come in and close the door, Cadence."

Cadence wasn't naïve. She knew what would happen if she did as he asked. Just as she knew there were a hundred – no, a *thousand* – reasons why she shouldn't.

She swallowed.

Hard.

And then she walked into the parlor…and closed the door.

A Note From the Author

I hope you enjoyed the time you spent with Evan (Wycliffe) and Hannah! From the very beginning their relationship was a bit of a role reversal – the woman chasing after the man instead of the other way around – and even though it wasn't at *all* how I set out to write it when I first started, I'm glad I listened to my characters and gave them the story they wanted.

As always, if you have a few minutes to spare **please leave a review**! Reviews are so incredibly helpful for independent authors like myself. Not only do I love reading them (yes, even the negative ones), but they also help other readers discover books they would have otherwise never heard about.

Printed in Great Britain
by Amazon